COLLINS
Workplace English

辦公室英語
實務篇

James Schofield

商務印書館

Collins 辦公室英語（實務篇）
Collins Workplace English (Practical Guide)

作　　者： James Schofield
責任編輯： 黃家麗
出　　版： 商務印書館（香港）有限公司
　　　　　香港筲箕灣耀興道 3 號東匯廣場 8 樓
　　　　　http://www.commercialpress.com.hk
發　　行： 香港聯合書刊物流有限公司
　　　　　香港新界大埔汀麗路 36 號中華商務印刷大廈 3 字樓
印　　刷： 中華商務彩色印刷有限公司
　　　　　香港新界大埔汀麗路 36 號中華商務印刷大廈 14 字樓
版　　次： 2015 年 1 月第 1 版第 1 次印刷
　　　　　©2015 商務印書館（香港）有限公司
　　　　　ISBN 978 962 07 0377 5
　　　　　Printed in Hong Kong
　　　　　版權所有　不得翻印

How to use 如何使用

建議用四十五分鐘至一個小時學習一個單元。全書合共二十四單元，每週抽出兩個小時學習，可於三個月內完成。

Step 1
先閱讀 Conversation 的英語對話。對話旁邊若標示了 ，請看相關視像。若標示了 ，請聆聽相關錄音。

Step 2
使用 Understanding 提供的內容，檢查自己是否已理解英語對話。

Step 3
嘗試回答 Practice 的練習題，並核對答案。

Step 4
按 Speaking 標示 You 的內容講英語，講完之後聆聽播音員的錄音，對比自己講的英語是否準確。

Step 5
參考 Resource bank 的實用資料，如 Translation of conversations、Key phrases for speaking、Key phrases for writing、On the phone — useful phrases、Grammar reference 等。

Contents 目錄

Resource Bank 參考資料

1 At reception 接待處

迎接訪客 | 詢問人名 | 填寫表格

Conversation

1 莎莉・史密夫是倫敦洛維工程公司的接待員，約翰・卡達和保羅・羅傑斯今天到訪這家公司。閱讀他們的對話，並且觀看短片。他們要跟誰見面呢？

Sally	**Good morning, how can I help you?**
John	Good morning. We're here to see Diane Kennedy at 10 o'clock.
Sally	**Can I have your names, please?**
John	Yes, it's John Carter and Paul Rogers from Australian Power Utilities. Here's my business card.
Sally	Thank you. **I'll just call Ms Kennedy.**
Paul	Thank you.
Sally	And **can you complete these security forms, please?**
Paul	Of course. Excuse me, can I have a pen?
Sally	Here you are. Diane? I have Mr Rogers and Mr Carter in reception for you. Right. Thank you.
Sally	Thank you. **Please could you wear these visitors' badges? Someone will come down to get you in a moment. Please have a seat.**
Paul	Thanks.
John	OK.

Did you know?

在日常英語對話裏，我們不會用二十四小時制。若想清楚表明是＂早上＂或＂中午＂，一般我們用 *am* 或 *pm*，或説 *in the morning*、*in the afternoon* 或 *in the evening*。

Understanding

2 再看一次，以下句子是正確 (T) 還是錯誤 (F)？

1 John and Paul work at Lowis Engineering.   T / F
2 Diane knows John and Paul are coming to see her.   T / F
3 John and Paul will have to wear badges.   T / F
4 John and Paul will have to wait a long time for Diane.   T / F

Key phrases

Dealing with visitors at reception

Good morning / afternoon / evening, … .	*Please could you wear this badge / these badges?*
How can I help you?	
Can I have your name(s), please?	*Someone will come down to get you.*
I'll just call Ms … .	*Please have a seat.*
Can you complete this form / these forms, please?	

Practice

3 將句內詞語排成正確順序。

1 evening, Good help I can how you

_____ ?

2 I Can names, your please have

_____ ?

3 Please you these complete could forms

_____ ?

4 will get come Someone down to you

_____ .

5 seat Please a have

_____ .

4 配對問題和答案。

Receptionist	**Visitor**
1 Good afternoon. How can I help you?	**A** Ali Khan.
2 Could you wear this badge, please?	**B** I'm here to see Diane Kennedy.
3 Can I have your name, please?	**C** Can you give me a pen?
4 Please can you complete this form?	**D** Of course.

5 看看約翰·卡達的名片，並填寫訪客表格的資料。

Lowis Engineering – Visitor Form

Surname / Last name _____

First / Given name _____

Company address _____

Email _____

Visiting _____

Time in _____ *9.30* _____ Time out _____

Signature *John Carter* _____

Australian Power Utilities

John Carter
Managing Director

Australian Power Utilities Inc
Block 7 Industrial Park
Canberra
Email: carter@apu.com

6 用你自己的資料，填寫訪客表格。

Language tip

表達時間

説 *nine o'clock* 或 *nine am* 表示早上九時；*a quarter past / after (US) eleven* 或 *eleven fifteen (am)* 表示早上十一時十五分；*half past two* 或 *two thirty (pm)* 表示下午二時三十分；*a quarter to eight* 或 *seven forty-five (pm)* 表示下午七時四十五分。

Speaking

01-02 CD

7 你是洛維工程公司的接待員，現在有一名訪客到訪。閱讀提示並接待訪客。播放 Track 01 並在呯一聲之後説話，由你先開始，然後聆聽 Track 02 完成對話。

You *Good morning madam, can I help you?*

Guest Yes, I have an appointment with Diane Kennedy for 11 o'clock.

You *(Ask her name.)*

Guest Jane Taylor from Taylor and Curtiss Consultants.

You *(Ask her to complete a security form.)*

Guest Can you give me a pen?

You *(Offer a pen.)*

Guest Thanks.

You *(Ask her to wear a visitor badge.)*

Guest Of course.

You *(Ask her to have a seat and say someone will come to get her.)*

Guest Good! Thanks for your help!

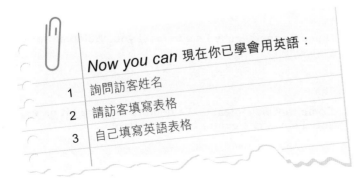

Now you can 現在你已學會用英語：

1 詢問訪客姓名
2 請訪客填寫表格
3 自己填寫英語表格

2　Company visitors 公司訪客

歡迎訪客來到公司　|　自我介紹　|　帶訪客到會面場地

Conversation

1 茉莉・歌文是黛安・甘迺迪在洛維工程公司的私人助理。她來到接待處和訪客見面。閱讀他們的對話，並且觀看短片。是誰叫茉莉和訪客見面呢？

Jasmine	**Excuse me, are you** John Carter and Paul Rogers?
John	Yes, we are. **I'm** John Carter and **this is** my colleague, Paul Rogers.
Jasmine	Hello, I'm Jasmine Goodman.
Paul	Hi.
John	Hi.
Jasmine	**Diane Kennedy asked me to meet you. Welcome to** Lowis Engineering.
Paul	Thank you.
John	Thank you.
Jasmine	**Come this way, please. We need to take the lift or, as you'd say, the elevator to the 3rd floor.**
Paul	It's a great building.
Jasmine	Yes, it is. It's a nice place to work.

Did you know?

美式英語用 *elevator* 表示 "電梯"，英式英語則用 *lift*。此外，美式英語用 *first floor* 表示 "一樓"，英式英語則用 *ground floor*。

Understanding

DVD

2 再看一次，用 *yes* 或 *no* 回答問題。

    1 Do John and Paul know Jasmine already?
    2 Does Jasmine work at Lowis Engineering?
    3 Do they need to take the lift?
    4 Does Jasmine like where she works?

Key phrases

Meeting company guests

Excuse me, are you ... ?	*Come this way, please.*
I'm ... / this is	*We need to take the lift / elevator / stairs to the 3rd floor.*
Diane Kennedy asked me to meet you.	
Welcome to	

Practice

3 連接句子的兩部份。

    1 Excuse me,   **A** to our company.
    2 I'm Paul and   **B** take the stairs to the 1st floor.
    3 Ms Kennedy asked   **C** are you Paul Rogers?
    4 Come this way,   **D** this is John.
    5 Welcome   **E** me to meet you.
    6 We need to   **F** please.

4 將句內詞語排成正確順序。

1 is my this John Carter I'm and colleague, Rogers Paul

_____.

2 floor We to take need the to lift the 3rd

_____.

3 Carter me, Excuse are Mr you

_____?

4 way, Come this please

_____.

5 Carter me asked Mr meet to you.

_____.

03
CD

5 茉莉・歌文正在接待處與另一位訪客見面。填空以完成句子，然後聆聽 Track 03 並核對答案。

Jasmine　(1) _____ me, (2) _____ you Ms Ringwood?

Guest　Yes, that's right.

Jasmine　I'm Jasmine Goodman. Diane Kennedy (3) _____ me to meet you.

Guest　Oh, hello Jasmine.

Jasmine　(4) _____ to Lowis Engineering.

Guest　Thank you!

Jasmine　This way, please. We (5) _____ to take the lift to the 3rd floor.

Guest　OK.

Language tip

與陌生人開始對話，或打斷某人說話時，可用 *Excuse me*。
表示樓層的數字可用序數：*first, second, third, fourth, fifth* 等。

Speaking

6 你在接待處和史頓遜先生見面。閱讀提示並歡迎他。播放 Track 04，並在呯一聲之後說話。由你先開始講，之後再聆聽 Track 05，對比你講的英語。

04–05
CD

> **You** *Excuse me, are you Mr Stenson?*
>
> **Visitor** Yes, that's right.
>
> **You** *(Give your name and say your boss, Mr Brown, asked you to meet him – welcome him.)*
>
> **Visitor** Thank you very much.
>
> **You** *(Ask him to follow you to the lift – you need to go to the 8th floor.)*
>
> **Visitor** Of course. This is a great building.
>
> **You** *(Say it's a nice place to work.)*

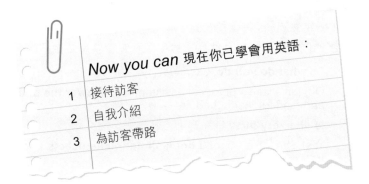

Now you can 現在你已學會用英語：

1　接待訪客
2　自我介紹
3　為訪客帶路

3 What do you do? 你做甚麼工作？

談你的工作 | 描述你的工作 | 詢問某人的工作

Conversation

1 茉莉・歌文要帶訪客約翰・卡達和保羅・羅傑斯到會議室，他們正在等候升降機。閱讀他們的對話，並且觀看短片，茉莉在會議裏要做甚麼？

John	So **what do you do**, Jasmine?
Jasmine	Oh, I'm Diane's personal assistant so **I answer the phone** and manage her schedule.
Paul	**Is she very busy** then?
Jasmine	Yes! She travels a lot. **I book all her plane tickets and hotels.**
John	I see. And **do you travel with her** sometimes?
Jasmine	No, not usually. I stay here and then **I'm responsible for** the office and **deal with** any problems.
Paul	You have a lot to do!
Jasmine	Yes. And in meetings, of course, **I take the minutes**.
Paul	... and **you look after visitors** to the company.
Jasmine	Yes, that's right! Ah, here it is. After you.
John	Thanks.

Did you know?

schedule 的發音，讀成 **sked**ule 或 **shed**ule 均可接受。美式英語讀作 **sked**ule，但英式英語中，兩個發音也有人用。

Understanding

DVD

2 再看一次，以下句子是正確 (T) 還是錯誤 (F)？

1 Jasmine has lots of different responsibilities. T / F
2 Jasmine usually travels with Diane. T / F
3 Jasmine runs the meetings. T / F
4 Jasmine helps the visitors. T / F

Key phrases

Asking about and describing responsibilities

What do you do?	*I answer the phone.*
Is (s)he / Are you busy?	*I reply to emails.*
Do you travel with her?	*I'm responsible for … .*
I'm a personal assistant / salesman / receptionist.	*I deal with … .*
	I take the minutes at meetings.
I book all her plane tickets / hotels.	*I look after guests / visitors.*

Practice

3 配對以下兩部份，組成正確詞組。

1 personal   A with
2 responsible   B to
3 take the   C minutes
4 look   D assistant
5 reply   E for
6 deal   F after

4 配對以下兩部份，組成完整句子。

1 I'm responsible   **A** after visitors to the company.
2 My colleague makes   **B** my work mobile after 6 o'clock.
3 The receptionist looks   **C** to my emails.
4 I always reply   **D** my flight reservations.
5 I don't answer   **E** for my boss's appointments.

5 按自己的工作情況完成以下句子。

1 I'm a _____ .
2 I'm responsible for _____ .
3 I look after _____ .
4 I reply to _____ .
5 I deal with _____ .

Language tip

當訪客詢問有關你的工作，盡量提供多些資料，令話題可以延續下去，盡可能回答完整句子，例如：Yes. And at meetings I take the minutes.，而不只是說 Yes, I do.。

Speaking

6 一位訪客詢問有關你的工作。播放 Track 06 並在嗶一聲之後開始說話，然後聆聽 Track 07，對比你講的英語。

06–07
CD

Visitor So, what do you do?

You *(Answer the question.)*

Visitor I see, that's interesting. Are you very busy?

You *(Answer the question.)*

Visitor And are you responsible for anything?

You *(Answer the question.)*

Visitor Do you do anything else?

You *(Answer the question.)*

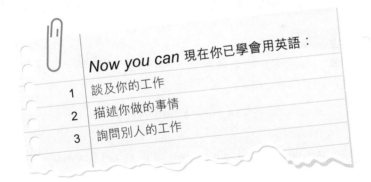

Now you can 現在你已學會用英語：

1 談及你的工作

2 描述你做的事情

3 詢問別人的工作

4　Making visitors feel welcome
令訪客覺得賓至如歸

照顧訪客　|　以茶點招待訪客　|　為延誤致歉

Conversation

DVD

1　茉莉・歌文將約翰和保羅帶到會議室。閱讀他們的對話，並且觀看短片，為甚麼茉莉會稱呼保羅為"羅傑斯先生"？

Jasmine	Here we are. **Can I take your coat?**
John	Thank you.
Jasmine	**Would you like to sit down? I'm afraid Diane is still in a meeting. Would you like a cup of coffee?**
John	Er ... .
Jasmine	Or a glass of water or juice?
John	I think I'd like some coffee, please.
Jasmine	**Would you like milk and sugar?**
John	Yes, please. Both. Thanks.
Jasmine	And **how about you**, Mr Rogers?
Paul	Please call me Paul. **I'd like some orange juice, please.**
Jasmine	**Here you are**, Paul.

Paul	Thanks very much.
Jasmine	**I'm sorry you have to wait, but Diane should be here soon.**
John	That's fine. Don't worry.

Did you know?

除了 *Don't worry* 之外，表達抱歉還有另一個方法，就是 *No problem*。澳洲人也常用 *No worries*。

用美式英語的人問你在咖啡要加甚麼時，通常問要不要加 *cream*，而不是加 *milk*。

Understanding

DVD

2 再看短片一次，以下句子是正確 (T) 還是錯誤 (F)？

1 Diane Kennedy is waiting for John and Paul in the meeting room.   T / F
2 Jasmine offers John and Paul something to drink.   T / F
3 Paul wants some coffee.   T / F
4 Jasmine is sorry because Diane is late.   T / F
5 John and Paul are angry that Diane Kennedy is late.   T / F

Key phrases

Polite offers and apologies

Can I take your coat(s)?	*How / What about you, ... ?*
Would you like to sit down / have a seat?	*I'd like some orange juice, please.*
I'm afraid that ... is (still) in a meeting.	*Here you are.*
Would you like some / a cup of coffee?	*I'm sorry you have to wait, but ... should be here soon.*
Would you like milk and sugar?	

3 將句中詞語排成正確順序。

1 tea you Would a like cup of

_____?

2 please like some I'd coffee,

_____.

3 you down like to Would sit

_____?

4 sorry to you I'm wait have

_____.

5 Carter here soon should Mr be

_____.

6 you sugar like milk Would and

_____?

7 afraid Mrs White I'm meeting is still in a

_____.

8 are you Here

_____.

4 配對句子。

1 Would you like to sit down?   A Just milk, please.
2 Would you like a cup of coffee?   B Thank you.
3 I'm sorry you have to wait.   C Please call me Paul.
4 Would you like milk and sugar?   D Don't worry.
5 What about you, Mr Rogers?   E No, but I'd like some water.

5 從方框選取詞語完成句子。

like	afraid	soon	have	here
please	should	in	take	some

1 I'm _____ Mr Carter is _____ a meeting.
2 Would you _____ to _____ a seat?
3 _____ you are.
4 Can I _____ your coat?
5 I'd like _____ coffee, _____.
6 Ms Goodman _____ be here _____.

Language tip

你向訪客提供茶點時，語氣必須友善熱情。你可以在問句最後提高聲調，例如：*Would you like a cup of coffee?* ↗

Speaking

08–09
CD

6 現在辦公室有兩位訪客，閱讀指示，招待客人直至你上司來到。播放 Track 8，在嗶一聲之後開口講話。由你先開始，然後聆聽 Track 09，對比你講的英語。

You	*(Ask if you can take the visitors' coats.)*
Visitor 1	Thank you.
Visitor 2	Here you are.
You	*(Offer them a seat.)*
Visitor 1	Thanks.
You	*(Ask if they want some coffee or juice.)*
Visitor 1	I'd like some coffee, please.
You	*(Ask what Visitor 2 – Mr Carter – would like.)*
Visitor 2	I'd like some orange juice.
You	*(Say your boss, Ms Kennedy, is in a meeting.)*
Visitor 1	No problem.
You	*(Say she will arrive soon.)*
Visitor 2	Thanks.

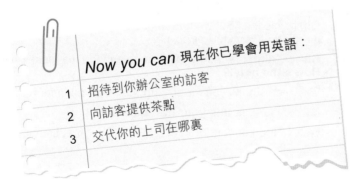

Now you can 現在你已學會用英語：

1 招待到你辦公室的訪客
2 向訪客提供茶點
3 交代你的上司在哪裏

5 Small talk 閒聊

主動攀談 | 檢查事情是否妥善處理 | 了解別人

Conversation

DVD

1 在等待上司黛安·甘迺迪來時，茉莉、約翰和保羅正在談話。閱讀他們的對話，並且觀看短片。黛安有沒有出席這次會議？

Jasmine	So, **how was your flight?**
John	Oh, it was fine. But we had to check in very early this morning at Frankfurt airport.
Jasmine	Oh yes, airport security takes such a long time these days. **How's the hotel?**
Paul	Very nice. Thank you for making the reservation for us.
Jasmine	My pleasure. **Is this your first time here?**
John	Well, not to London, of course. But it's our first time to your company.
Paul	Yes. And we're very interested in your products.
Jasmine	Good. **How long are you staying in** London?
Paul	A week. **What should we do** at the weekend?
Jasmine	Mmm ... **do you like** football? You know, soccer?
John	Yes, very much.

Jasmine	**Would you like to** see a Chelsea match this weekend? I could get you some tickets.
Paul	Thank you, that's a great idea!
John	Fantastic!
Jasmine	You're welcome. By the way, I've made reservation for lunch for you and Diane at a French restaurant near here. Is that OK?
John	Excellent! Thank you.
Paul	That sounds great.
Jasmine	Good. Well, **I'll find out where Diane is and let her know you're here**.
Paul	Fine.

Did you know?

美式英語 *soccer* 在英式英語相等於 *football*（足球），而美式英語的 *football*，則相等於 *American football*（美式足球）。

Understanding

DVD

2 再看一次，然後回答問題。

1 Where did John and Paul fly from?
2 Who made the hotel reservation for John and Paul?
3 Have they been to Lowis Engineering before?
4 What does Jasmine offer to organize for the weekend?
5 Where will they have lunch today?

Key phrases

Making small talk

How was your flight / trip / journey?	*Do you like … ?*
How's / How is the hotel?	*Would you like to … ?*
Is this your first time here?	*I'll find out where … is and tell her / him you're here.*
How long are you staying in … ?	
What should we do … ?	

Practice

3 連接句子的兩部份。

1	How was	A	where Mr Brown is.
2	How is	B	time in Paris?
3	Is this your first	C	the hotel?
4	How long are	D	your flight?
5	Do you	E	do in the evening?
6	What should we	F	you staying in Berlin?
7	I'll check	G	like Italian food?

4 按答句寫出合適的提問。

1 _____ No, I often come here.

2 _____ It's very comfortable. And close to the centre!

3 _____ Terrible. The weather was bad.

4 _____ Theatre? Yes, I do. Very much.

5 _____ 'The Lion King'? Yes, I would.

6 _____ Only three days, unfortunately.

Speaking

5 和倫敦來的訪客閒聊，閱讀指示，在你上司來到之前和訪客談話。播放 Track 10，並在嗶一聲之後説話，由你先開始。然後，聆聽 Track 11，對比你講的英語。

10–11 CD

You	*(Ask about the flight from London.)*
Visitor	Oh, not very good. The weather in London is terrible at the moment. It's nice to see some sunshine here.
You	*(Agree. Ask about her hotel.)*
Visitor	It's very nice. Thank you for organizing it.
You	*(Reply then ask if she has visited your town before)*
Visitor	Yes, this is my first time. What should I do in the evening?
You	*(Ask if she likes your country's food.)*
Visitor	Very much!
You	*(Ask if she wants to try a local restaurant this evening.)*
Visitor	Oh, yes! Very much. Thank you.
You	*(Reply. Then ask how long she is staying in your town.)*
Visitor	Until Friday. Then I fly back to London.
You	*(Offer to go to find your boss.)*
Visitor	Thanks a lot.

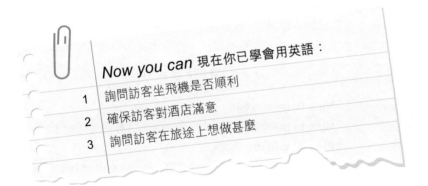

Now you can 現在你已學會用英語：

1 詢問訪客坐飛機是否順利
2 確保訪客對酒店滿意
3 詢問訪客在旅途上想做甚麼

6　Introductions 互相介紹

互相介紹　|　認識別人　|　直呼名字

Conversation

DVD

1　茉莉・歌文找到她的上司黛安・甘迺迪，然後帶她和兩位訪客見面。閱讀他們的對話，並且觀看短片。為甚麼黛安沒有向保羅和約翰介紹茉莉？

Jasmine	Here she is! Diane, **I'd like to introduce** John Carter and Paul Rogers from Australian Power Utilities.
Diane	**Nice to meet you!**
John	**Nice to meet you too**, Ms Kennedy. I'm John Carter.
Diane	**Please, call me** Diane!
John	**Fine**, Diane. **And I'm** John. **This is my colleague** Paul Rogers.
Paul	**Pleased to meet you**, Diane.
Diane	**Pleased to meet you too**, Paul. And **I see you've met my assistant Jasmine already**. I'm very sorry I'm late. I'm afraid my last meeting went on for a while.
John	Oh, don't worry. Jasmine took care of us.
Diane	Good. So, please have a seat.
Paul	Thanks.

Did you know?

第一次見面時可以向人說 *How do you do?*，不過這樣說較為正式，雖然此句句尾有問號，但它並非一個提問。

Understanding

DVD

2 再看短片一次，以下句子是正確 (T) 還是錯誤 (F)？

1 John and Paul have met Diane before.   T / F
2 Diane is very apologetic about being late.   T / F
3 Diane was in a long meeting.   T / F
4 Diane asks John to use her first name.   T / F

Key phrases

Introductions

I'd like to introduce ... from ...?	*This is my colleague ... .*
Nice to meet you.	*Pleased to meet you.*
Nice to meet you too.	*Pleased to meet you too.*
Please, call me ...	*I see you've met ... already.*
Fine. And I'm ...	

Practice

3 將句中詞語排成正確順序。

1 to John meet Nice you,

_____.

2 is Diane colleague, This Kennedy my

_____.

3 meet to you Nice too

_____.

4 Carter see you've already my manager I John met

_____.

5 Ms to meet you, Pleased Goodman

_____.

6 Jasmine me call Please

_____.

4 填空完成句子。

1 Fine. And _____ Paul.

2 I see you've met Diane _____ .

3 This _____ my _____ John.

4 Nice to meet you _____ .

5 I'd _____ to _____ Paul Rogers from APU.

6 Please _____ me Paul.

5 將句子排列成正確順序以完成對話。播放 Track 12 並且核對答案。

	Mr Kline	OK, but it was a bit late taking off.
	Diane	Nice to meet you, Mr Kline.
	Mr Kline	Nice to meet you too. But please call me Mike.
1	Jasmine	Diane, can I introduce you to Mr Kline?
	Mr Kline	Thank you.
	Mr Kline	No, thanks.
	Diane	So how was your flight?
	Diane	And would you like some coffee?
	Diane	Of course. And I'm Diane. Would you like to take a seat?

Language tip

每次總是要肯定已向訪客介紹過房間內的每個人，留意黛安説 *And I see you've met my assistant Jasmine already.*，以確認她的助手已獲介紹。

Speaking

6 你現在和你公司的一位訪客見面，你的同事正在介紹你。播放 Track 13，在呸一聲之後説話，然後聆聽 Track 14，對比你講的英語。

13–14
CD

Colleague	So here we are! I'd like to introduce Lee Toms from DPU.
You	*(Greet Mr Toms.)*
Lee	Nice to meet you too but please call me Lee.
You	*(Tell him your first name and ask him to take a seat.)*
Lee	Thank you.
You	*(Apologize for being late.)*
Lee	No problem.
You	*(Offer coffee.)*
Lee	No, thanks.
You	*(Ask about Lee's journey.)*
Lee	It was fine. No problems.

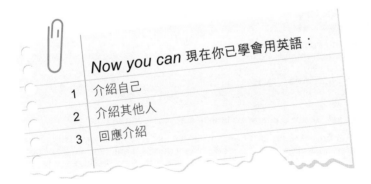

Now you can 現在你已學會用英語：

1　介紹自己
2　介紹其他人
3　回應介紹

7　An inquiry by email 用電郵查詢

撰寫正式電郵　|　表達請求　|　查詢資料

Email

1　洛維工程公司的茉莉・歌文正要籌辦一個會議。她向誰寫電郵？

From:　　jasmine.goodman@lowis.com
To:　　　info@anchorhotels.co.uk
Date:　　February 7
Subject:　Event for Lowis Engineering

Dear Sir or Madam

I am writing to ask about conference facilities at your London hotel.

On May 3, Lowis Engineering is organizing an event for 500 major customers. **We would like to** demonstrate some of our equipment and present information about our products to our guests. **Please let me know if** your conference facilities are available on this date.

I would be grateful if you could send me information about the presentation equipment, room sizes and catering facilities in your hotel. **Please include** a telephone number and a contact person I can call to discuss details.

I look forward to hearing from you.

Yours faithfully

Jasmine Goodman
Lowis Engineering

Did you know?

在美式英語裏，若不知道所寫電郵要發給誰，會以 *To Whom It May Concern* 作開首，*Best regards* 作結束。在英式英語裏，則以 *Dear Sir or Madam* 作開首，*Yours faithfully* 作結束，如上述例子一樣。

Understanding

2 再讀電郵一次，為每條問題選出最適當的答案 A、B 或 C。

1 Lowis Engineering is organizing a conference for:

   A tourists in London

   B company staff

   C people it does business with

2 May 3 is the date when:

   A Jasmine is writing the email

   B the conference will take place

   C the hotel says the conference can take place

3 Jasmine wants:

   A the name of somebody at the hotel

   B to visit the hotel

   C to check the costs

Key phrases

Asking for information

I am writing to ask about … .	*I would be grateful if you could … .*
We would like to … .	*Please include … .*
Please let me know if … .	*I look forward to hearing from you.*

Practice

3 連接句子的兩部份。

1 Please let me know   **A** to ask you about your prices.

2 I would be grateful if   **B** like to organize an event.

3 I am writing   **C** if you can meet me.

4 I look forward to   **D** a photograph of the facilities.

5 We would   **E** meeting you soon.

6 Please include   **F** you could organize a meeting.

4 將句中詞語排成正確順序。

1 your include address Please number telephone and

_____.

2 like would to We to invite you presentation a

_____.

3 I be grateful could you if send brochure us would a

_____.

4 let me is know for this time you possible Please if

_____.

5 I forward look to Tuesday seeing on you

_____.

5 閱讀茉莉發給活動籌辦公司的電郵，找出每題的錯處，並且改錯。

Dear Sir or Madam

(1) I writing to ask if you can organize an event for us in London.
(2) On May 3, Lowis Engineering is organize an event for approximately 500 major
(3) customers and business partners. We will like to demonstrate some of our
    equipment and present information about our products to our guests.
(4) Please lets know if this date is possible.
(5) I could be grateful if you could send me information about your services
    and
(6) prices. Please includes a telephone number and a contact person I can
    call.
(7) I look forward to hear from you.

Your faithfully

Jasmine Goodman

Language tip

用現在進行式描述現時正在做的事，例如：*I am writing to ask about...*。談將來的計劃時，可用 *On May 3, Lowis Engineering is organizing...*。

在正式電郵裏，不該使用縮寫，而該用全寫，例如：*I am writing...* 並非 *I'm writing...*；該用 *I would be grateful...* 並非 *I'd be grateful...*。

參閱 165 頁找到更多關於現在進行式的資料。

Writing

6 你的上司祖安娜·添士，要你寫一封電郵，嘗試用筆記幫助自己。你任職於基頓汽車租賃公司。

Write to the Event Manager, Carlton Hotel.
We need a large room for our Annual General
Meeting in New York:
Date: April 19
Numbers: 300 guests
We need information about:
1) Room size
2) Presentation equipment
3) Catering
4) Costs

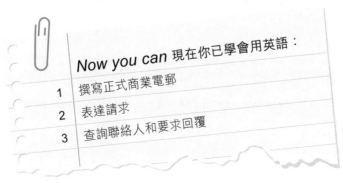

Now you can 現在你已學會用英語：

1 撰寫正式商業電郵

2 表達請求

3 查詢聯絡人和要求回覆

8　A reply to an inquiry 回覆查詢

寄出資料　|　描述特別優惠　|　提供合約詳情

Email

1　安佳酒店的莊・馬田寫了一封電郵給茉莉・歌文，向她提供會議設施的資料。他提及了哪個特別優惠？

From:　　j.martin@anchorhotels.co.uk
To:　　　jasmine.goodman@lowis.com
Date:　　February 8
Subject:　Re: Event for Lowis Engineering

Dear Ms Goodman

Thank you for your email of February 7. **With reference to your** request for conference facility information, **please find attached** a PDF file with a description of our London hotel. The information can also be seen online at www.Anchorhotels.com.

I am pleased to inform you that we are offering a discount of 25% for any reservation made before the end of February. We still have rooms available for the date of your conference, May 3.

If you would like further information about our services, **please contact me on** 020 8307 4001.

Yours sincerely

Jon Martin
Conference Manager – Anchor Hotels

Did you know?

在美式英語裏，01/03/2012 表示 2012 年 1 月 3 日。
而在英式英語裏，01/03/2012 表示 2012 年 3 月 1 日。
為免引起誤解，可以拼寫月份，例如：March 1, 2012；February 7, 2014。

Understanding

2 再讀電郵一次，以下句子是正確 (T) 還是錯誤 (F)？

1 Lowis Engineering is organizing a conference for February 7.   T / F
2 The hotel information can only be found on the website.   T / F
3 If Jasmine makes a reservation before March 1, she can get a discount.   T / F
4 The hotel is fully booked on May 3.   T / F
5 Jon Martin is the conference manager at Anchor Hotels.   T / F

Key phrases

Giving information

Thank you for your email of … .	*We are offering a discount of … .*
With reference to your … .	*If you would like further information about … .*
Please find attached / enclosed … .	
I am pleased to inform you that … .	*Please contact me on … .*

Practice

3 從方框選取詞語完成句子。

> available   conference facilities   contact
> discount   price information   email

1 Our company is offering a _____ of 10%.
2 Thank you for your _____ of October 19.
3 Please find enclosed _____ for our conference rooms.
4 With reference to your request for _____ information, please find attached a brochure as a PDF file.
5 Please _____ me on 0207 98 5151.
6 I am pleased to inform you that we have a meeting room _____ on March 27.

4 將句中詞語排成正確順序。

1 you 0207 98 5151 like further on would information, If contact me

_____.

2 the am inform pleased to you that this date is available I

_____.

3 morning Thank your for you phone call this

_____.

4 find service our information Please attached

_____.

5 reference of to 27 your With email March

_____.

5 這封電郵由另一家酒店發給茉莉・歌文，將句子排成正確順序。

Dear Ms Goodman

Please find enclosed information about our conference equipment and prices. [ ]
With reference to the date of your event, we have rooms available at that time. [ ]
Yours sincerely [ ]
If you would like further information, please let me know. [ ]
Thank you for your phone call to my assistant this afternoon. [1]
We are pleased to inform you that we have a special offer for catering facilities in May. [ ]

Yours sincerely

Priti Makesch

Language tip

如果你經常要寫內容相近的電郵，可用幾個關鍵詞作為範本，再按不同情況稍為修改。

Writing

6 你在一家酒店工作。播放 Track 15，並且聆聽上司法蘭·史丁給你的電話留言，再完成這封給顧客的電郵。

15
CD

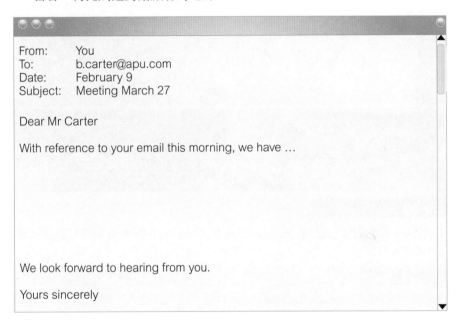

From: You
To: b.carter@apu.com
Date: February 9
Subject: Meeting March 27

Dear Mr Carter

With reference to your email this morning, we have …

We look forward to hearing from you.

Yours sincerely

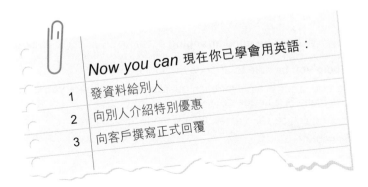

Now you can 現在你已學會用英語：

1 發資料給別人

2 向別人介紹特別優惠

3 向客戶撰寫正式回覆

9 A follow-up email 跟進電郵

撰寫非正式電郵 | 提出請求 | 請求幫助

Email

1 茉莉·歌文寫電郵給莊·馬田，談及洛維公司的活動。茉莉請莊做多少件事呢？

From: jasmine.goodman@lowis.com
To: j.martin@anchorhotels.co.uk
Date: March 20
Subject: Lowis event on May 3

Dear Jon

Can you help me? Would you mind arranging a visit for my manager, Diane Kennedy, to see your conference facilities at the hotel? She wants to see what they are like. **Would you be able to** arrange this for next week?

Secondly, **could you** arrange a gift for each guest at the event? **Are you able to** do this for less than €50 per guest?

If that is OK, then could you send a new offer with the total price?

Many thanks for your help.

Best wishes

Jasmine

PS I can't open the pictures of the conference rooms you sent. **Please advise.**

Did you know?

無論給相熟或不相熟的人發電郵，也可在電郵結尾用 *Best wishes* 或 *Best Regards*。

Understanding

2 再讀電郵一次，為每條問題選出最合適的答案 A、B 或 C。

1 This email is informal because:
   A it's short
   B Jasmine uses Mr Martin's first name
   C Jasmine uses a PS at the end

2 Diane Kennedy wants to:
   A test the conference facilities
   B go to the Anchor Hotel
   C cancel the event

3 Jasmine wants Jon:
   A to buy her a gift
   B to buy one gift for all the guests
   C to buy one gift for each guest

4 The present should cost:
   A under €50
   B over €50
   C €50

5 Jasmine is having problems:
   A with a document Jon sent
   B with some photos Jon sent
   C with some video Jon sent

Key phrases

Asking for help

Can you help me?	*Could you ...?*
Would you mind +ing ...?	*Are you able to ...?*
Would you be able to ...?	*Please advise.*

3 連接句子的兩部份。

1	Are you able to	A	reply to this email?
2	Can you help me	B	me as soon as possible?
3	Would you mind	C	able to meet me?
4	Could you contact	D	helping me?
5	Would you be	E	send a new offer?

4 將句中與請求有關的詞語排成正確順序。

1 the tomorrow you to Are come to able meeting

_____?

2 you sending possible mind a new contract as Would as soon

_____?

3 you to translation send the Paul Could Rogers

_____?

4 be you able Would to me help

_____?

5 you by Friday finish the Can report

_____?

5 按照你本星期的工作，填寫三至五項一定要做的事。

1 _____

2 _____

3 _____

4 _____

5 _____

你從明天開始放假，但你的工作還沒有完成，請求一位同事協助。

Could you _write the meeting report?_

Are you able to _____?

Would you mind _____?

Would you be able to _____?

Language tip

請求別人做一件困難的事時，可用 *Would you mind + ing...?* 記得每次使用時，動詞要加 *ing* 形式，例如：*Would you mind organizing / calling / visiting / presenting...*。

回應 *Would you mind...?* 的請求時，可用 *No, not at all.* 或 *Of course not.*。

Writing

6 莊‧馬田想請他的助手凱蒂‧鍾斯帶黛安‧甘迺迪參觀安佳酒店，完成他寫給凱蒂的電郵。

From:　　j.martin@anchorhotels.co.uk
To:　　　k.jones@anchorhotels.co.uk
Date:　　March 28
Subject:　Visit from important customer tomorrow

Dear Katy

Tomorrow, Diane Kennedy from Lowis Engineering is coming but I'm not well so can you (1) _____ me? She is arranging an event on May 3 so could you (2) _____ her the conference facilities?

Also, are you (3) _____ to take her to lunch? I want her to see how good the catering is.

Finally, would you (4) _____ showing her the gifts we plan for the guests at the event? Her assistant, Jasmine Goodman, ordered them.

Is this OK with you? Please (5) _____ if there is any problem.

Best wishes

Jon

Now you can 現在你已學會用英語：

1　寫非正式的商業電郵
2　解釋你的需要
3　為某事請求協助

10　A reply to a follow-up email
回覆跟進的電郵

撰寫非正式的回覆 ｜ 建議 ｜ 提供協助

1　莊·馬田是安佳酒店的會議設施經理，他給洛維工程公司的茉莉·歌文發
電郵，提出了一些建議。他提出了多少個建議？

From:　　j.martin@anchorhotels.co.uk
To:　　　jasmine.goodman@lowis.com
Date:　　March 21
Subject:　Lowis event on May 3

Dear Jasmine

Thanks for your email and your requests. I have put my answer after your
questions:

1) Would you mind arranging a visit for my manager, Diane Kennedy?
Not at all. **If you like, we could** give Ms Kennedy a tour of the facilities
and offer her lunch.

2) Could you arrange a gift for each guest at the event?
Yes, no problem. **What about including** a personal card from you or Ms Kennedy with the gift?
3) Are you able to do this for less than €50 per guest?
Of course. **Why don't you look** at the attached list of possible gifts and tell me what you think is best?
4) Could you send a new offer with the total price?
Yes. I haven't finished the new offer yet, but I will do it tomorrow. **Would you like me to** send it to Ms Kennedy as well?
5) I can't open the pictures of the conference rooms you sent.
Have you tried opening the pictures in Microsoft PowerPoint? Or **should I** send you the photos in the post?

I hope these suggestions help. **Let me know if you need anything else.**

Best regards

Jon

Did you know?

你可以直接在原來收到的電郵之下加評論或回覆，可用不同顏色或加上你姓名的首字母以茲識別。

Understanding

2 再讀電郵一次，回答以下問題。

1 When Diane visits the Anchor Hotel in central London, what will Jon offer her?
2 What does Jon suggest including with the guests' gifts?
3 Why does Jasmine ask for a new offer?
4 What does Jon offer to send Jasmine in the post?

Key phrases

Making suggestions	Offering help
What / How about +ing ... ?	*If you like, we could ... .*
Why don't you ...?	*Would you like me to ...?*
Have you tried +ing ... ?	*Should I ...?*
	Let me know if you need anything else.

3 將句中詞語排成正確順序。

1 don't you a meeting Why arrange

_____?

2 you like me to send an Would email

_____?

3 you offices moving Have tried

_____?

4 What meeting of about the time the changing

_____?

5 me Let know if date you another need

_____.

6 I appointment change the Should

_____?

4 一位同事跟你説，他因工作太多未能完成報告。按你所想，給他提一些建議以完成句子。

1 What about _____?

2 How about _____?

3 If you like, I could _____ .

4 Let me know if you need _____ .

5 Why don't you _____?

5 閱讀莊的助手凱蒂·鍾斯的電郵，在每題找出錯處並且改錯。

Dear Jon

(1) Here are few suggestions for the Lowis Web event we're organizing in May in the central London hotel.

(2) Who don't we use the conference rooms next to the bistro on the top floor?

(3) The view of London is great. And how about have a celebrity chef for the catering?

(4) My sister works with a celebrity chef and, if you like, he could ask how much it costs to hire him for the day.

(5) Also, have you thought about organize some music? It would be nice for the breaks, I think.

(6) Would you like me check the prices for a band?

(7) Let me know if you needs anything else.

Regards

Katy

Language tip

談及過去已完成但與現在有關的事情時,可以用現在完成式,例如:*I have put my answers after your questions*。在這種情況下,絕不會用固定時間表達式如 *yesterday / last year* 等。

有關現在完成式的資料,可參閱 169 頁。

Writing

6　一位同事想安排一個辦公室派對,發一封電郵給她,並提出一些建議,可以用下面的筆記幫助自己。

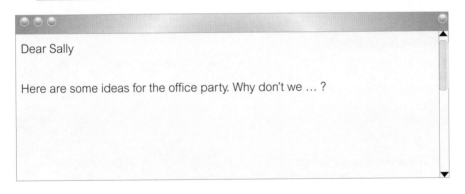

Place – use company cafeteria, comfortable
Time – start 6 pm, finish midnight – need to work next day!
Music – live band. Offer to contact friend in band 'The Big Noise'?
Anything else?

Dear Sally

Here are some ideas for the office party. Why don't we … ?

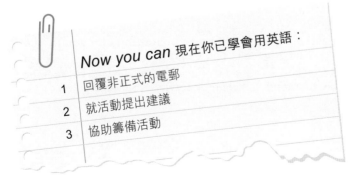

Now you can 現在你已學會用英語:

1　回覆非正式的電郵
2　就活動提出建議
3　協助籌備活動

11 Invitations 邀請

撰寫邀請信 | 描述活動 | 提供活動資料

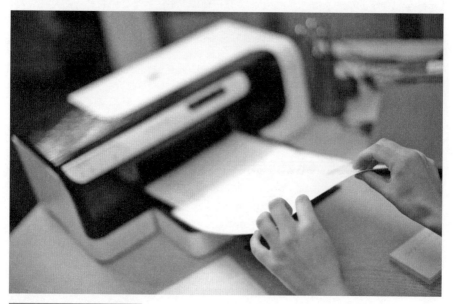

Emails

1 茉莉・歌文邀請不同人士參加她為洛維公司籌辦的活動。以下兩封電郵有甚麼分別？

A

Dear Mr Cao

I am writing on behalf of Diane Kennedy, Sales Director for Lowis Engineering. **We would like to invite you to** our *Lowis event* on Thursday May 3 from 12 pm to 6 pm, followed by dinner, at the Anchor Hotel, London.

At the event, we are presenting our newest products to our major customers and partners. **It will be an opportunity for you** to meet and talk to our top engineers and designers.

Please find attached an agenda for the day and the venue. **We hope you are able to attend** and **we look forward to meeting you** on May 3.

Yours sincerely

Jasmine Goodman

B

Dear John

Diane **asked me to write to you**. On May 3 we are organizing a **Lowis event** for our major customers and partners to present our latest products at the Anchor Hotel, London. It starts at noon and there will be a dinner in the evening. **Are you free on this date**, and **would you and Paul like to come**?

The agenda for the day and the location details are attached. **I hope to see you on** May 3.

Best wishes

Jasmine

Did you know?

在英式英語裏，用 *noon* 或 *midday* 表示"中午"。

Understanding

2 再讀電郵一次，以下句子是正確 (T) 還是錯誤 (F)？

1 Jasmine is writing for Diane.   T / F
2 The event is for the whole day.   T / F
3 After the event, the visitors can do something together.   T / F
4 In the second email, Jasmine only invites John.   T / F

Key phrases

Invitations

I am writing on behalf of … . (formal)	*X asked me to write to you. (informal)*
We would like to invite you to … . (formal)	*Are you free on this date / at this time / in June? (informal)*
It will be an opportunity for you … . (formal)	
We hope you are able to attend … . (formal)	*Would you like to come? (informal)*
We look forward to meeting you / seeing you there. (formal)	*I hope to see you on … . (informal)*

3 將句中詞語排成正確順序。

1 Chairman It will an to our opportunity be for you meet

_____.

2 Thursday like to would invite you meeting to a on We

_____.

3 lunch you like Would to to come

_____?

4 hope able you We are to conference attend the

_____.

5 Are o'clock free at 6 meeting you for a

_____?

4 你在寫信給你的同事，邀請他週末一起吃晚飯。電郵內有些短語太正式，請將每題改為較非正式的用法。記得在某些情況之下，問句可以用來提出建議。

Dear Marcus

We would like to invite you
and Sally to dinner on Saturday.
I've asked Janette and Freddy
too so it should be good. [1]   1 _____?

We hope you are able to attend
and we look forward to meeting
you then. [2]   2 _____.

Yours sincerely [3]   3 _____.

Katy

Language tip

表示月份或季節時，應在前面使用 *in*，例如：*in January*，*in the summer*。
表示星期時，應在前面使用 *on*，例如：*on Saturday*。
表示準確時間時，應在前面使用 *at*，例如：*at six o'clock*。
表示公眾假期時，應在前面使用 *at*，例如：*at Christmas* (time)。
表示週末時，英式英語是 *at the weekend*，美式英語則是 *on the weekend*。

Writing

5 你的老闆，祖安娜・添士想你邀請一位重要客戶見面和共晉午餐。參考你老闆寫的筆記來撰寫邀請函。

Please write to Helmut Probst, Order Manager at Tycoil Electronics. Invite him to our key customer meeting Thursday morning, April 7. I want him to meet our Managing Director, Tim King, and the sales team.
Then I will take him to lunch at the Ritz.
Thanks!

Joanna – Sales Director, CMCX Ltd

Now you can 現在你已學會用英語：

1 撰寫正式和非正式的電郵邀請

2 描述活動

3 向別人提供資料

12 Replies to invitations 回覆邀請

接受邀請 | 拒絕邀請 | 給予原因

Emails

1 閱讀以下三封電郵，都是回覆茉莉・歌文發出的邀請。誰接受了邀請？
誰又拒絕了？

A

Dear Ms Goodman

Thank you for your invitation to my manager, Mr Cao, for the event at Lowis Engineering on May 3. Mr Cao **is pleased to accept your invitation** and will attend from 12.00 until 18.00 and the dinner event at the Anchor Hotel.

Yours sincerely

Jenny Chang

B

Dear Ms Goodman

With reference to your email of March 7, **unfortunately Ms Schmidt is unable to attend** the Lowis Engineering event on May 3 **due to** a business trip on that date.

We wish you success with your event.

Best regards

Eva Fleck

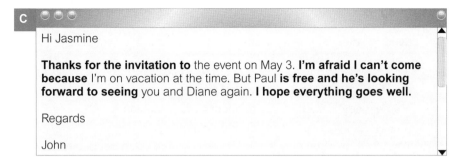

C

Hi Jasmine

Thanks for the invitation to the event on May 3. **I'm afraid I can't come because** I'm on vacation at the time. But Paul **is free and he's looking forward to seeing** you and Diane again. **I hope everything goes well.**

Regards

John

Understanding

2 再讀電郵一次，找出符合以下描述的人：

1 is on holiday on May 3.

2 will come to all of the Lowis event.

3 is on a business trip.

4 is looking forward to seeing Jasmine and Diane.

Key phrases

Accepting or declining an invitation

Thank you for your invitation to … . *Thanks for the invitation to … .*	*Unfortunately, XYZ is unable to attend … due to … .*
XYZ is pleased to accept your invitation.	*I'm afraid I can't come because … .*
XYZ is free and is looking forward to seeing … .	*We wish you success with your event.*
	I hope everything goes well.

Practice

3 再看 Key phrases 表格內的短語一次，在短語旁寫上相應的英文字母，(F) 代表正式，(I) 代表非正式。

4 從方框選取詞語完成句子。

attend	due	free	because of	pleased	success

1 Mr Carter is unable to _____ the conference.
2 I wish you _____ with your workshop.
3 Ms Kennedy is _____ to accept your invitation.
4 This is _____ to another appointment.
5 I'm _____ on May 3 and I'm looking forward to being there.
6 I can't be there _____ a business trip.

5 將句中詞語排成正確順序。

1 you for on invitation Thank the the to Friday meeting
_____ .

2 hope goes everything We on Friday well
_____ .

3 to Goodman a business Ms Due is attend unable trip to due
_____ .

4 Mr invitation Rogers your pleased to is accept
_____ .

6 你的同事獲供應商邀請出席銷售會議，以了解供應商的最新產品。她寫了一封電郵，並請你替她檢查。標示的部份過於非正式，請替她重寫，使語氣更正式。

Dear Mr Hunter

Thanks a lot for the invitation to your sales conference on September 12. [1]
Unfortunately, I am unable to attend due to a business trip.
But my colleague, Jasmine Goodman, is free and will be there. [2]
I hope everything goes well. [3]

Regards [4]

1
2
3
4

Language tip

當你未能接受邀請時，總要説明原因，例如：*due to a business trip* 或 *because I'm on holiday* (英式) / *vacation* (美式) 。另外，可以用 *unfortunately* 或 *I'm afraid* 使你的原因聽起來更有禮貌。

Writing

7 你獲邀出席一個週年慶祝活動，嘗試回覆邀請，説明接受邀請或解釋不能出席的原因。

Dear Mr Rogers

We would like to invite you to our company's **25th Anniversary** on Thursday July 6 from 6 o'clock until midnight, followed by fireworks.

Please find attached information about the day. We hope you are able to attend and we look forward to seeing you on July 4.

Yours sincerely

Katy Jones

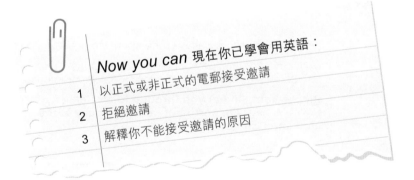

Now you can 現在你已學會用英語：

1 以正式或非正式的電郵接受邀請

2 拒絕邀請

3 解釋你不能接受邀請的原因

13　Incoming calls 來電

接聽電話 | 解釋某人不在 | 回覆電話

Telephone calls

16 CD

1 聆聽 Track 16 的兩段電話對話，找出阿倫想找哪個部門？為甚麼黛安不能接聽電話？

A

Sally	Lowis Engineering, Sally Tyrone speaking. Can I help you?
Alan	Hello, this is Alan Jay from Texas Consultants. I'd like to speak to somebody in your Sales Department, please.
Sally	**Please hold. I'll put you through to** Ms Kennedy. ... Hello, Mr Jay? **I'm sorry but her line's busy at the moment. Can you hold?**
Alan	Er, yes, OK.
Sally	**I'm afraid she's still engaged. Can you call back later?**
Alan	Hm. All right. Goodbye.
Sally	Goodbye.

B

Jasmine	Diane Kennedy's phone, Jasmine Goodman speaking.
John	Hello, Jasmine. John Carter from APU here. Is Diane there?

Jasmine	Oh hi, John. **I'm afraid she's not available at the moment.** She's in a meeting.
John	Oh, I see. I need to speak to her today.
Jasmine	Well, the meeting is until 11 o'clock. Can you call back later?
John	Yes, OK. **I'll call back at** 11.30. Is that OK?
Jasmine	Yes, that's fine.
John	Good. Thanks, Jasmine. Bye.
Jasmine	Bye, bye John. **Maybe speak to you later.**

Did you know?

有時你可以直接打通某人在某公司的電話。但有時卻要接待員或接線生轉駁電話。

Understanding

16
CD

2 再聽一次，為每條問題選出最適合的答案 A、B 或 C。

1 Alan can't speak to Diane because:
  A she isn't there
  B she doesn't want to speak to him
  C she's talking to somebody else on the phone

2 Sally asks Alan:
  A to hold on to the phone
  B to wait for a moment
  C to put the phone down

3 John wants to:
  A visit Diane today
  B speak to Diane today
  C have a meeting with Diane

4 John says:
  A he will call back
  B send an email
  C wait for a call from Diane

Key phrases

Dealing with calls

Please hold.	*Can you call back later?*
I'll put you through to … .	*I'm afraid she's not available at the moment.*
I'm sorry but her line's busy at the moment.	
Can you hold?	*I'll call back at … .*
I'm afraid she's still engaged (UK) / on the line (US).	*(Maybe) speak to you later.*

Practice

3 連接句子的兩部份。

1 I'll put you through	**A** you later.
2 Can you	**B** available at the moment.
3 I'll call back	**C** to Jasmine Goodman.
4 I'm afraid she's not	**D** still on the line.
5 I'm afraid she's	**E** hold?
6 Speak to	**F** hold.
7 Please	**G** this afternoon.

4 將句中詞語排成正確順序。

1 sorry moment busy but Mr at I'm Carter's line is the

_____ .

2 boss later will My call back

_____ .

3 afraid on a he's business I'm trip

_____ .

4 you back morning call Can tomorrow

_____ ?

5 put through the you to Sales I'll Department

_____ .

5 按右欄的回應，在左欄寫出句子。

1 _____ OK. I'll call back after lunch then.

2 _____ She's in a meeting? How long for?

3 _____ The Sales Department? Yes, thank you.

4 _____ No, I can't hold. I'll call back later.

5 _____ Still engaged? OK, I'll hold.

Language tip

用 *will* 表示決定做某事，例如：*The phone's ringing! — Don't worry, **I'll** answer it!*；
***I'll** call back at 11:00.*
參閱 168 頁以了解更多資料。

Language tip

如果說一位同事無法接聽電話，替他道歉和解釋他在做甚麼是有禮貌的做法，例如：*I'm afraid he's in a meeting / on a business trip.*

Speaking

6 一位顧客打電話來找你同事。播放 Track 17，然後在呸一聲之後說話，再聆聽 Track 18，對比你講的英語。

17–18 CD

Customer	Can I speak to Mr Rogers, please?
You	*(Tell him Mr Rogers is in a meeting.)*
Customer	Oh, I see. Well, can I speak to Pauline Coates in the Sales Department?
You	*(Tell him you will put him through.)*
Customer	Thanks.
You	*(Apologize and tell him that Ms Coates' line is busy.)*
Customer	Oh, I see.
You	*(Ask if he wants to hold.)*
Customer	Hmm, I don't think so.
You	*(Ask if he can call back later.)*
Customer	Yes, OK, thank you. Bye.
You	*(Say goodbye.)*

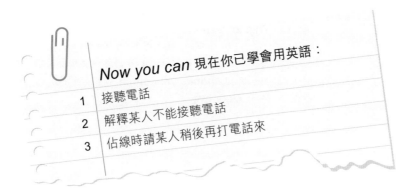

Now you can 現在你已學會用英語：

1 接聽電話
2 解釋某人不能接聽電話
3 佔線時請某人稍後再打電話來

14 Outgoing calls 打電話

請求找某人談 | 確認電話號碼 | 感謝別人

Telephone calls

19
CD

1 洛維工程公司的茉莉・歌文要打電話給三個人，確認會議的安排。聆聽 Track 19 她講的話。她能否找到她要找的人？

A	
Jasmine	Ah, good morning. **Could I speak to Alan Jay, please?** ... He's in a meeting. OK, I'll call back later. ... Is 12 o'clock OK? ... Great! **Can you give me his extension number, please?** ... 8 – 6 – 5 –1. Well, **many thanks for your help!**

B	
Jasmine	**Hi, I'd like to speak to Andrea Schmidt, please.** ... Hello, Ms Schmidt. **This is Jasmine Goodman calling from** Lowis Engineering. ... **I'm calling about** our meeting next Wednesday in London. **I just want to check** if that is OK for you. ... Good. Well, **thanks very much**, Ms Schmidt. ... See you next week. Goodbye.

C

Jasmine

Hello, my name's Jasmine Goodman from Lewis Engineering. **Can you put me through to** Mr Johansson, please? ... Oh, on a business trip? ... Um ... can you give me his mobile number, please? ... 00 49 1552 8896441. And can you give me his land line number also? ... I see, so that's 00 49 899 315 96021. ... All right. Well, **thanks a lot**.

Did you know?

英式英語用 *mobile phone* 表示 "手機" ，美式英語則用 *cell phone* 。
一般來説，在美式英語裏，你會將 0 説成 *zero* ，在英式英語裏則説成 *Oh* 。

Understanding

2 再聽一次，然後回答問題。

19
CD

1 Does Jasmine have Alan's direct telephone number?
2 What reason does Jasmine give for calling Ms Schmidt?
3 Why can't Mr Johansson speak to Jasmine?

Key phrases

Making telephone calls

Could I speak to XYZ, please?	*I'm calling about ... .*
Hi, I'd like to speak to XYZ, please.	*I just want to check ... .*
This is XYZ calling from	*Many thanks for your help!*
Can you give me his extension number, please?	*Thanks very much.*
	Thanks a lot.
Can you put me through to ...?	

Practice

3 配對提問 / 陳述和答覆。

1 Can you give me his extension?
2 Well, thanks very much!
3 Could I speak to Ms Kennedy?
4 I'd like to speak to Mr White.
5 I'm calling about our meeting today.
6 This is Paul Rogers calling from APU.

A My pleasure.
B What time today?
C It's 4155.
D Hi, Paul!
E I'll put you through to him.
F I'm afraid she's in a meeting.

4 將句中詞語排成正確順序。

1 you to Can me through put James please Harris,

_____ ?

2 calling month about I'm the conference next

_____ .

3 I number flight want to check just your

_____ .

4 you mobile give Mr Can Carter's me number

_____ ?

5 I Please speak to could White Kate

_____ ?

6 Anthony much very Well, thanks

_____ .

5 茉莉打電話給身在巴黎的安東・威茲，想確認他會否出席洛維工程公司的會議。將句子排成正確順序來組成一段對話，再聆聽 Track 20 核對答案。

20
CD

1	Jasmine	Could I speak to Mr White, please?
	White	Hello, Jasmine.
	Jasmine	Oh, good! Well, thanks a lot, Mr White and see you next week. Bye.
	White	Anton White.
	Jasmine	Hi Mr White, this is Jasmine Goodman calling from Lowis Engineering.
	Jasmine	I'm just calling about the meeting next Tuesday at 10 o'clock. I just want to check if the time is OK for you.
	Receptionist	I'll put you through.
	White	The time is fine. No problem at all.
	Jasmine	Bye.
	White	See you then. Bye.

Language tip

談到電話號碼時，需要一個個數字講，例如3156 是 *three one five six*。如果兩個相同號碼放在一起，可以分開講，或用 double 表示，例如 004 是 *zero zero four* 或 *double oh four*。55 是 *double 5*。

如果想結束一段電話對話，可以用 *Well*，接着用 *thank you* 讓對方知道你已經講完，例如：*Well, many thanks for your help!* 或 *All right. Well, thanks a lot!*

Speaking

21–22
CD

6 你嘗試打電話給酒店的聯絡人安排一次會面。播放 Track 21 並在呷一聲之後説話，再聆聽 Track 22，對比你講的英語。

Receptionist Apelles Hotels, how can I help you?

You *(Give your name and company and ask to speak to Cindy Fox.)*

Receptionist I'll put you through. ... Oh, I'm sorry she's on a business trip.

You *(Ask for Ms Fox's mobile phone number.)*

Receptionist Yes, of course. It's 0155 289 6645.

You *(Repeat the number, thank the receptionist and say goodbye.)*

Receptionist Goodbye.

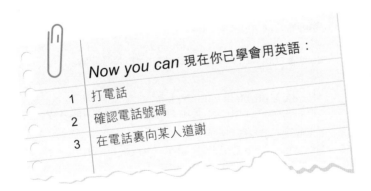

Now you can 現在你已學會用英語：

1 打電話
2 確認電話號碼
3 在電話裏向某人道謝

15 When things go wrong 事情出錯時

查詢送遞 | 處理送遞的問題 | 查詢資料

Telephone calls

23 CD

1 茉莉‧歌文要打電話給供應商 "班治到會公司",再打電話給包裝速遞公司 TPS,聆聽 Track 23,以下出現了哪兩個問題?

A	Benji's	Benji's Catering, can I help you?
	Jasmine	Yeah, this is Jasmine Goodman from Lowis Engineering. I'm calling about an order for food I made for today.
	Benji's	Yes?
	Jasmine	**There's a problem with** the lunchtime special executive menu for ten I ordered. **You sent the wrong delivery**.
	Benji's	What did you receive?
	Jasmine	Er, let me see the delivery note. Ah yes, the children's party special.
	Benji's	Ah, I see.
	Jasmine	**Could you pick it up** from our office?
	Benji's	Yes, of course.
	Jasmine	And **can you give us a refund**, please? We really don't need the lunch special now.

B TPS		Thank you for calling TPS. To arrange a pickup, press 1. For the latest information on a package sent with TPS, press 2.
Tony		TPS, good morning. This is Tony speaking, how can I help you?
Jasmine		Oh, hi. My name's Jasmine Goodman. **It's concerning** a package I sent to Singapore. **Something's gone wrong with** the delivery. It hasn't arrived yet.
Tony		OK. Can I have your tracking number, please?
Jasmine		Er, it's MU 76344 HJ.
Tony		Let me just check for you. ... Yes, sorry to keep you waiting. I'm afraid it's been delayed. It's in the Singapore depot at the moment. Apparently, there was a problem with the delivery address.
Jasmine		Oh, really? **What's happened to** it?
Tony		It seems the house number didn't exist. Can I check it with you? Was it to 40 Golden Orchard Road?
Jasmine		No, 14!
Tony		Right – one four. I see.
Jasmine		**Can you tell me when it'll be delivered?**
Tony		We'll put it on a truck right away so it will arrive today. I sincerely apologize for any inconvenience.

Did you know?

電話錄音的目錄裏，有時需要按 hash (#)、pound (£) 或 star (*) 鍵。

Understanding

2 再聽兩段對話一次，以下句子是正確 (T) 還是錯誤 (F) ？

23
CD

1 Jasmine didn't make an order to Benji's Catering.	T / F
2 Jasmine wants Benji's to pick up the order.	T / F
3 Jasmine wants money back from Benji's.	T / F
4 Jasmine is waiting for a package from Singapore.	T / F
5 The package is still in London.	T / F
6 TPS had the wrong address.	T / F

Describing problems and asking for information

There's a problem with … .	*Could you collect it / pick it up … ?*
It's concerning … .	*Can you give us a refund?*
You sent the wrong delivery / order.	*What's happened to … ?*
Something's gone wrong with … .	*Can you tell me when it'll be delivered?*

Practice

3 連接句子的兩部份。

1	Something's gone wrong	**A**	to our order?
2	What's happened	**B**	the delivery.
3	Can you give	**C**	up the package?
4	There's a problem with	**D**	with the reservation.
5	Could you pick	**E**	me a refund?

4 將句中詞語排成正確順序。

1 you package me when Can you will collect the tell

_____ ?

2 equipment our order concerning for It's office

_____ .

3 the delivered wrong with package Something is you

_____ .

4 my concerning LO 743 KL package, tracking It's number

_____ .

5 our happened to What's delivery

_____ ?

6 sent to the company wrong You delivery our

_____ .

5 先看右欄的回應，再在左欄寫出相關句子。可以用 Key phrases 內的短語。

1 _____ arrive?　　The truck is on its way to you now, sir.

2 Can you _____ ?　　Yes, of course. How much did you pay?

3 _____ it up?　　No problem. When is a good time?

4 What's _____ ?　　Can I have your tracking number, please?

5 _____ wrong _____ .　　Oh, what did we send?

Language tip

24 CD

與商業伙伴交流時，小心使用以下容易混淆的數字。聆聽以下各組數字。
13 – 30 14 – 40 15 – 50 16 – 60 17 – 70 18 – 80 19 – 90
確保發音清晰，如果不確定對方所說的話，小心查證以免出錯。

24 CD

以下是一個方法，可幫助你記得發音相似的英文字母。聆聽以下字母的讀音。

A H J K	O
B C D E G P T V Z（美式）	Q U W
F L M N S X Z（英式）	R
I Y	

Speaking

25–26 CD

6 你打電話向供應商投訴送遞服務。播放 Track 25 ，在嗶一聲之後講話，再聆聽 Track 26，對比你講的英語。

Supplier	Jackson Office Supplies. How can I help you?
You	*(Give your name and company. Say you have a problem with an order you made last week.)*
Supplier	I'm sorry to hear that. Can you give me the order number?
You	*(JYG 723 / 19 / BP. Say they sent the wrong ink for the printers.)*
Supplier	Oh, I see.
You	*(Ask them to pick up the wrong ink and bring the right ink – TP2000.)*
Supplier	No problem.
You	*(Ask when they will come.)*
Supplier	I think tomorrow should be possible. Is that OK?
You	*(Say that's OK and goodbye.)*

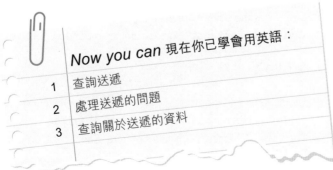

Now you can 現在你已學會用英語：

1 查詢送遞

2 處理送遞的問題

3 查詢關於送遞的資料

16 Telephone messages 電話留言

寫下留言 | 給別人留言 | 確認資料

Telephone calls

1 茉莉‧歌文本週要替她的上司接聽電話。聆聽 Track 27 三段電話錄音。黛安在哪裏？

27
CD

A	Jasmine	Jasmine Goodman.
	Alan	Good morning, Jasmine. This is Alan Jay from Texas Consultants. I'd like to speak to Diane Kennedy, please.
	Jasmine	I'm afraid she's away this week, Mr Jay. **Can I take a message**?
	Alan	Yes. Can you tell her I'm flying to London next week and I'll see her at the sales conference?
	Jasmine	**Can I just check that?** You're coming to London next week and you'll see her at the sales conference.
	Alan	Yes, that's right.

B	Jasmine	Hello, Jasmine Goodman.
	Tina	Hi, Tina Jones here, Jasmine. Can I speak to Diane, please?
	Jasmine	I'm sorry, Ms Jones, but she's not here. She's back on Monday next week.

Tina	OK. Well, **could you take a message?**
Jasmine	Yes, of course.
Tina	Tell her I can come to the meeting on the 14th and that my colleague, Marco Toncini, is coming too. But we won't get to you until 10 o'clock. Our flight from Milan only arrives at 8.30.
Jasmine	All right, **let me repeat that**: you and Mr Toncini will be at the meeting on the 14th from 10 o'clock. Is there anything else I can help you with?

C

Jasmine	Jasmine Goodman.
Mark	Hello, Jasmine. It's Mark Pole here.
Jasmine	Hi, Mark.
Mark	Is Diane in the office?
Jasmine	She's on holiday this week, Mark. **Do you want to leave a message for her?**
Mark	Well, you can tell her I called, but I also want to send her an email. Could you give me her email address?
Jasmine	Yes, of course. It's diane.kennedy@lowis-engineering.com.
Mark	**I'll read that back to you**: diane dot kennedy at lowis hyphen engineering dot com.
Jasmine	Right. And I'll tell her you called.

Did you know?

電郵地址裏的符號讀法如下：

1) "@" 讀作 at　　　　3) "." 讀作 dot
2) "-" 讀作 hyphen　　4) "_" 讀作 underscore。

Understanding

2 再聽一次，在茉莉寫給黛安的留言裏找錯處。

27
CD

Telephone message 1
From: Alan Jay　　To: Diane Kennedy
Mr Jay is flying to Liverpool next month and will see you at the sales conference.

Telephone message 2
From: Tina James　　To: Diane Kennedy
Ms James is coming to the meeting on the 4th with her colleague Marco Toncini. She'll arrive at 10 o'clock.

Telephone message 3
From: Mark Pole　　To: Diane Kennedy
Mark called. He is sending you something in the post.

Taking and leaving a message

Can I take a message?	Can I just check that?
Could you take a message?	Let me repeat that: ...
Do you want to leave a message for her?	I'll read that back to you: ...

Practice

3 將句中詞語排成正確順序。

1 Can for I Carter leave message a Mr

_____ ?

2 you me message like to leave him Would a

_____ ?

3 message read you the back I'll to

_____ .

4 take you Goodman a message Could for Jasmine

_____ ?

5 I information just check Can the

_____ ?

6 Rogers want you leave a Do message for Mr to

_____ ?

4 約翰‧卡達想請茉莉給黛安一個留言，聆聽 Track 28 完成表格。

Telephone message

From: John Carter   To: Diane Kennedy

Date: May 4

_____

_____

_____

Language tip

如果不肯定資料正確，別害怕請對方重複。講話時應該緩慢而清晰，尤其是重複數字和名字的時候。

Speaking

29–30
CD

5 你接聽了一位顧客的電話，對方想找你上司談，你要寫下他的留言。播放 Track 29，在嗶一聲之後說話，再聆聽 Track 30，對比你講的英語。

Customer	Can I speak to Mr Rogers, please?
You	*(Say you're sorry but he's in a meeting.)*
Customer	Oh, I see. I have some information for him.
You	*(Ask if you can take a message.)*
Customer	Um...yes, OK. Can you tell him that my conference in June is cancelled? If he wants to speak to me about it, he can call me on my new mobile. The number is 01521 300 9957.
You	*(Say that you want to check the information. Repeat the information and the mobile phone number.)*
Customer	That's right. Thanks very much. Goodbye.
You	*(Say goodbye.)*

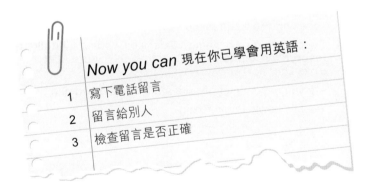

Now you can 現在你已學會用英語：

1 寫下電話留言

2 留言給別人

3 檢查留言是否正確

17 Conference arrangements 會議安排

訂會議室 ｜ 查詢設備 ｜ 安排茶點

Telephone call

1 茉莉打算在酒店籌辦一個大型商務會議，聆聽她 Track 31 的電話對話。
參加者將在哪裏吃午飯？

Cindy	Apelles Hotel Reservation Department, Cindy Fox speaking. How can I help you?
Jasmine	Good morning. My name's Jasmine Goodman. **I'd like to reserve a room for a** meeting from 9 o'clock until 6 o'clock for next Friday, April 27th.
Cindy	Are you a customer of ours already, Ms Goodman?
Jasmine	Yes. It's Lowis Engineering.
Cindy	All right. How many participants will there be?
Jasmine	20 to 25.
Cindy	OK, let me check. ... Yes, that's fine, Ms Goodman. The Napoleon and the Wellington Suites are both available.
Jasmine	Excellent. I'd like the Wellington Suite, please. Now, **does the room have a** projector?
Cindy	Yes, and Internet. Is there anything else you need?
Jasmine	**Could you provide a** flipchart and four pinboards?
Cindy	Yes.

Jasmine	Good. Now, **can you set up a coffee break** for 10.15, and another break for 4.30, please?
Cindy	OK. What about water and juice during the meeting?
Jasmine	Oh, good idea! Next, lunch: **Please could you reserve tables in the hotel restaurant** for 1 o'clock?
Cindy	Certainly, Ms Goodman.
Jasmine	Good. Now, **would you mind repeating that back to me**?
Cindy	Of course. Friday 27th, the Wellington Suite from 9.00 until 6.00 for 20 to 25 people. Coffee at 10.15, lunch at one, and a coffee break again at 4.30, plus water and juice in the meeting room.
Jasmine	And **don't forget the** equipment!
Cindy	One projector, one flipchart and three pinboards.
Jasmine	No. One projector, one flipchart and four pinboards.
Cindy	Sorry, got that. I'll confirm it all in an email to you.
Jasmine	Thanks. My email address is … .

Did you know?

英式英語用 *pinboard* 表示 "佈告板"，美式英語則用 *bulletin board*。

Understanding

2 再聽一次，以下句子是正確 (T) 還是錯誤 (F)？

31
CD

1 Jasmine wants to reserve a room for a conference.   T / F
2 The Wellington Suite has a projector for presentations.   T / F
3 Jasmine doesn't want any other presentation equipment.   T / F
4 Jasmine arranges an afternoon break for 3.30 pm.   T / F
5 The meeting will last all day.   T / F

Key phrases

Making a hotel reservation for a meeting

I'd like to reserve / book a room for a … .	*Please could you reserve / book tables in the hotel restaurant?*
Does the room have a … ?	*Would you mind repeating that back to me?*
Could you provide a … ?	
Can you organize / set up a coffee break for … ?	*Don't forget the … .*

3 從方框選擇詞語完成句子。

| reserve | forget | mind | projector | provide |

1 Can you set up a _____ in the room?
2 Could you _____ coffee and tea at about 4 o'clock?
3 Would you _____ repeating that back to me?
4 I'd like to _____ a conference room, please.
5 Don't _____ the pinboards!

4 將句中詞語排成正確順序。

1 you tables us reserve Please could some for

_____?

2 like I'd to reserve tickets some

_____.

3 you me repeating Would that to mind back, please

_____?

4 the connection room Does have Internet an

_____?

5 organize next a meeting you Can for week

_____?

5 播放 Track 32 ，聆聽另一位顧客和仙迪·霍斯的對話，完成預約表格。

32
CD

Apelles Reservation Form

Customer name: _____ Company: Topaz Lighting

Date: _____ Time: _____

Meeting room: Napoleon Suite

Participant numbers: _____

Equipment required: _____

Refreshments: Coffee break +

Time required: _____

Language tip

打電話預約時，用 *I'd like to reserve...* ，然後用 *Could you ... ?* 或 *Can you ... ?* 提出特定要求，例如：*Could you provide tea and coffee?*。
當用電話安排預約時，最好向對方取得書面確認，例如：*Could you confirm the details in an e-mail?*

Speaking

33–34
CD

6 你要代表公司打電話給仙迪·霍斯訂房。播放 Track 33，在嗶一聲之後說話，再聆聽 Track 34 完成對話，對比你講的英語。

Hotel　Apelles Hotel reservation department, Cindy Fox speaking. How can I help you?

You　*(Give your name and company. Say you want to reserve a meeting room for July 30, 10.00 – 3.00.)*

Hotel　All right. For how many participants?

You　*(Say 14.)*

Hotel　Yes, that's fine. The Napoleon Suite is available.

You　*(Ask if the room has an Internet connection.)*

Hotel　Yes, it does. Is there anything else you need?

You　*(Ask if the hotel could provide a multimedia projector and flip chart.)*

Hotel　No problem. What about refreshments?

You　*(Say you would like sandwiches and coffee at 12.00.)*

Hotel　Fine. I'll confirm this in an email.

You　*(Say thanks and goodbye.)*

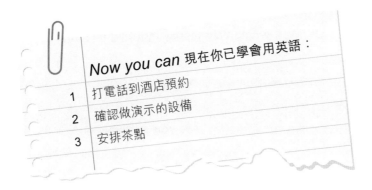

Now you can 現在你已學會用英語：

1　打電話到酒店預約
2　確認做演示的設備
3　安排茶點

18 Travel plans 旅遊計劃

安排會議 | 確認對方是否有時間 | 同意一個方便的時間

Telephone calls

35
CD

1 茉莉・歌文要替她上司黛安・甘迺迪安排與在格但斯克的彼得・華西維奇見面。茉莉打電話給他，聆聽 Track 35 兩人的對話，找出會面的時間。

Jasmine	Diane is flying to Warsaw the day after tomorrow and visiting Gdansk next week. **Would it be possible for her to see you** then, Mr Wasilewski?
Peter	Hmm, I'm quite busy, but I'm sure we can find time.
Jasmine	I see. **Do you have time on** Tuesday afternoon at 2 pm?
Peter	Er, no. I'm afraid I have a meeting from 2 until 6 o'clock.
Jasmine	OK. Well, **would Wednesday morning be convenient** for you?
Peter	Ah, I'm sorry but I have an appointment at the dentist at 9.00. Is Ms Kennedy available on the day after? I mean Thursday?
Jasmine	Oh sorry, no, I'm afraid not. She has to be back in London by noon on Thursday. **Are you available on** Wednesday afternoon?
Peter	Hmm, let me see. Yes, I can do that.

Jasmine	Excellent! So, **could you meet Ms Kennedy at** 2.30 in your office? **Does that work for you?**
Peter	Yes, that's fine. I look forward to seeing her then.
Jasmine	Thanks very much. I'll tell her. Bye.
Peter	Bye.

Did you know?

一般來説，可以用 *Ms* 尊稱已婚或未婚女士，或用 *Mrs* 尊稱已婚女士。在英語裏，稱呼男性沒有明顯分別，尊稱男士總是用 *Mr*。

Understanding

35
CD

2 再聽一次，為每條問題選出最適合的答案 A、B 或 C。

1 Peter Wasilewski's office is in:

A London

B Warsaw

C Gdansk

2 Mr Wasilewski's Tuesday afternoon meeting finishes:

A at some time before 6.00

B at 6.00

C after 6.00

3 Diane is coming back to London:

A no later than 12.00 on Thursday

B not before 12.00 on Thursday

C on Thursday afternoon

Key phrases

Asking for an appointment

Would it be possible for her to see you then / on … / at … ?	*Are you / Is she available tomorrow / on Thursday?*
Do you have time on Friday / next Tuesday?	*Could you meet her at 4.30?*
Would Monday / Thursday be convenient for you?	*Does that work for you?*

Practice

3 連接句子的兩部份。

1	Are you available	**a**	11.30?
2	Would Tuesday morning	**b**	time on Friday?
3	Could you meet Mr Carter at	**c**	on Tuesday morning?
4	Would it be possible for	**d**	Mr Rogers to see you?
5	Do you have	**e**	be convenient for you?

4 將句中詞語排成正確順序。

1   10.30 you Does work for

_____?

2   Would Kennedy lunchtime, be you convenient Ms for

_____?

3   be it possible Would for him to me see tomorrow

_____?

4   John morning available on Is Monday

_____?

5   you to Jasmine meet quarter at Could four

_____?

5 茉莉打電話給在華沙的伊娃·米斯奇維斯，替黛安預約見面時間。將句子排成正確順序以組成一段對話，再聆聽 Track 36 核對答案。

36
CD

1	Jasmine	… Diane will be flying to Warsaw on Monday. Do you have time on Monday?
	Eva	Sure. That would be fine.
	Jasmine	Well, are you available on Monday evening? Ms Kennedy would like to take you to dinner.
	Eva	Well, after 10.00 perhaps.
	Eva	That's very kind, but I have another appointment in the evening.
	Eva	On Monday? Hmm, that's difficult.
	Jasmine	Mmm, well, would Tuesday morning be convenient for you?
	Jasmine	Great! How about 11 o'clock? Does that work for you?

Language tip

用 *until* 描述一個動作的完成時間，例如：*I've got a meeting from 2 until 6 o'clock*，即是會議在兩點鐘開始，六點鐘結束。

用 *by* 描述一個動作最遲開始的時間，例如：*She has to be back in London by noon on Thursday*，即星期四中午十二點鐘是黛安最遲回到倫敦的時間。

Speaking

37–38
CD

6 你打電話給一位客戶預約時間見面。播放 Track 37，然後在呸一聲之後說話，再聆聽 Track 38，對比你講的英語。

Customer	So you are flying to Madrid next week? Hmm, when can we meet?
You	*(Ask if he is free on Tuesday.)*
Customer	Tuesday? No sorry, I'm away on a business trip.
You	*(Ask about Wednesday morning.)*
Customer	I'm afraid Wednesday morning is no good. I have to go to the doctor.
You	*(Ask about Wednesday afternoon.)*
Customer	Um ... yes ... I think so.
You	*(Suggest 3 o'clock.)*
Customer	Is a little later possible?
You	*(Suggest 4 o'clock at the latest because you have to leave by 6.00.)*
Customer	Yes, that's fine. I'll see you then!

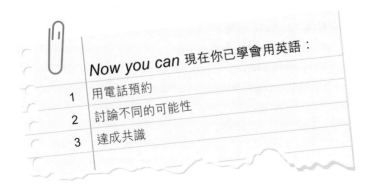

Now you can 現在你已學會用英語：

1 用電話預約
2 討論不同的可能性
3 達成共識

19　Welcome back 歡迎回來

問候認識的人 ｜ 送禮物 ｜ 感謝某人送的禮物

Conversation

DVD

1 約翰・卡達和保羅・羅傑斯回到洛維工程公司。茉莉到接待處和他們見面。閱讀他們的對話，並且觀看短片。保羅送了甚麼禮物給茉莉？

Jasmine	Jasmine Goodman. Hello, Sally. ... John Carter and Paul Rogers? Yes, that's fine. I'll come and get them. ... Great, thanks very much, Sally.
Paul	Jasmine, **good to see you again**!
Jasmine	Hello, Paul. Hi, John. **Nice to see you again too**!
John	**How are you**, Jasmine?
Jasmine	**I'm fine, thanks. And you?**
John	**Very well, thanks**.
Jasmine	Have you checked into your hotel OK?
John	Yes, we have.
Jasmine	Good, good.
Paul	Thank you for organizing everything for us again.
Jasmine	No problem.

Paul	And **this is a small present from our company** to say thank you for all your help.
Jasmine	... **Oh, thank you very much! That's really kind of you!**
Paul	No worries.
Jasmine	I'll open it upstairs. Ready to go up?
Paul	Yeah.

Did you know?

在某些文化裏，馬上拆開禮物是不禮貌的。

Understanding

DVD

2 再看一次，以下句子是正確 (T) 還是錯誤 (F) ？

1 John and Paul come up to Jasmine's office by themselves.   T / F
2 Jasmine knows John and Paul already.   T / F
3 John and Paul needed to make a hotel reservation.   T / F
4 Jasmine is pleased with her present from John and Paul.   T / F
5 Jasmine opens her present immediately.   T / F

Key phrases

Greeting acquaintances, giving and receiving a gift

Good to see you again!	*Very well, thanks.*
Nice to see you again too!	*This is a small present from ... .*
How are you?	*Thank you very much! That's really kind of you.*
I'm fine, thanks. And you? / How about you?	

Practice

3 配對以下句子。

1 That's really kind of you!   A Thank you very much. It's lovely!
2 How are you?   B Nice to see you again too!
3 Good to see you again!   C Fine thanks, Jasmine. And you?
4 This is a gift from our country.   D You're welcome.

4 將句中詞語排成正確順序。

1 really you kind That's of

_____ .

2 to again Diane see you Nice too,

_____ .

3 Tony are How you,

_____ ?

4 a us small of present from Here's all

_____ .

5 thanks. about you And Fine, how

_____ ?

5 閱讀茉莉和安佳酒店的莊・馬田的對話。在每題找出錯處，然後更正。

1	Jon	Hello Jasmine. Good too see you again! _____
2	Jasmine	Hello, Jon. Nice to see you again to! _____
3	Jon	How is you? _____
4	Jasmine	Fine, thank. And you? _____
5	Jon	Very while, thanks. _____
	Jasmine	Good.
6	Jon	Thanks four using Anchor Hotels for your conference. _____
7	Jasmine	Mine pleasure. _____
8	Jon	And these is a small present from Anchor Hotels. _____
9	Jasmine	Oh, thank you very much! That are really kind of you! _____
10	Jon	Not it all. _____

Language tip

別人感謝你時，可使用以下其中一句回應：
My pleasure.
You're welcome!
Not at all!
No worries. (非正式)

Speaking

6 你看到來自另一個國家的同事歌倫，播放 Track 39 ，在呯一聲之後講話。
再聆聽 Track 40，對比你講的英語。

39–40
CD

Colin	Hello! Good to see you again!
You	*(Reply.)*
Colin	How are you?
You	*(Say you're fine and ask about him)*
Colin	Very well. And thank you so much for arranging my hotel room.
You	*(Reply.)*
Colin	And here is a small thank-you present for all your hard work.
You	*(Reply.)*
Colin	My pleasure!

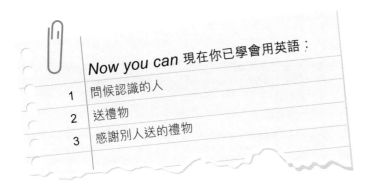

Now you can 現在你已學會用英語：

1 問候認識的人
2 送禮物
3 感謝別人送的禮物

20　Plans 計劃

解釋日程表 ｜ 描述一系列的活動 ｜ 談將來的計劃

Conversation

DVD

1　茉莉替約翰‧卡達和保羅‧羅傑斯草擬了一個日程表。閱讀他們的對話，
並且觀看短片。約翰曾和誰見面？

Jasmine	So, here's the schedule for the next two days. Can I just run through it?
John	Yes, of course.
Jasmine	All right. **First of all,** this afternoon you're meeting Chris Fox, the factory manager, together with Diane. They want to show you the factory.
Paul	Interesting.
Jasmine	**After** Chris has given you the tour, Diane wants to show you some of our ideas for the new equipment and you can talk to some of our engineers. **And then** Diane is taking you to dinner, together with Mr Harris, the Managing Director of Lowis Engineering.
John	Sounds good.
Jasmine	**Next,** tomorrow morning at 9.30, Diane and I are picking you up from your hotel to take you by car to our test facility just outside of London and you can see some of our equipment in action.

Paul	That'll be interesting.
Jasmine	I hope so. **While** you're there, you're meeting the test manager, Jim Gibson, and he can show you everything.
John	Great, I know Jim already, in fact.
Jasmine	Ah, good. **Finally**, at about 4 o'clock a taxi's picking you up from here and taking you to the airport. Your flight back to Australia is at 7 o'clock, I think.
Paul	Yes, that's right. Well, that all sounds very well organized. Thanks again, Jasmine.
Jasmine	You're welcome.

Understanding

DVD

2 再看短片一次，替約翰和保羅完成以下的日程表。

> **Today**
> 11.00 am – <u>arrive Lowis Engineering</u>
> 1.00 pm _____
> 3.00 pm _____
> 6.00 pm _____
>
> **Tomorrow**
> 9.30 am _____
> 4.00 pm _____
> 7.00 pm – <u>flight to Sydney</u>

Key phrases

Outlining a schedule

First of all, ...	Next, ...
After / After that	While ... .
And then	Finally, ...

3 用方框內的詞語填空，以完成關於籌辦成功會議的文章。

after   finally   first   next   then   while

Did you know that the average business person sits in meetings for 190 hours every year? That's eight days! So how can you organize effective meetings? (1) _____ of all, think: is a meeting necessary? (2) _____ you have decided it is necessary, don't invite too many people. More than seven and good discussion is difficult.

(3) _____ you must plan the agenda carefully and (4) _____ send it in time for people to prepare. (5) _____ the meeting is running, make sure that there is coffee and water for everybody. (6) _____, check that everybody has ... .

4 將句中詞語排成正確順序。

1 I'm to Today listen to to my, English work CD while planning driving

_____.

2 all, meeting we're having First a of

_____.

3 that, I'm lunch with having After Jasmine

_____.

4 writing for boss Then a report, I'm my

_____.

5 this a evening I'm going to Finally, movie

_____.

5 參考你下星期的日記，寫下你的計劃。

First of all, on Monday I'm _____.
After / After that, on Tuesday _____.
And then on Tuesday afternoon _____.
Next, on Wednesday _____.
Finally, on Friday _____.

Language tip

談及將來一些確定的計劃時，可用現在進行式，例如 *This afternoon you're meeting Chris Fox.*
參考 165 頁，了解更多現在進行式的資料。

Speaking

6 一個重要客戶沙地女士明天將到公司來，你的經理要求你向她解釋日程表。用以下內容幫助自己，播放 Track 41，並在嗶一聲之後説話，再聆聽 Track 42，對比你講的英語。

41–42
CD

> **Tomorrow**
> 10.00 am – pick up Ms Sahdi at airport, show her the new office
> 11.00 am – meeting Ms Sahdi, you and sales team
> 1.00 pm – take Ms Sahdi to lunch
> 3.00 pm – visit factory and explain about new equipment
> 7.00 pm – go to theatre and have dinner

Manager	Ah, there you are. Can you tell me about my schedule for tomorrow with Ms Sahdi?
You	*(First of all, at 10.00 you're picking up Ms Sahdi at the airport and ... .)*
Manager	I see. What next?
You	*(Next, at 11.00 ... .)*
Manager	Very well. And then?
You	*(And then, ...)*
Manager	I see. After that?
You	*(After that, ...)*
Manager	Good! Anything else?
You	*(Finally, ...)*

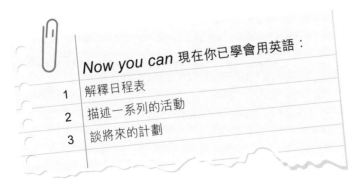

Now you can 現在你已學會用英語：

1　解釋日程表
2　描述一系列的活動
3　談將來的計劃

21 A change of plan 改變計劃

更改安排 │ 道歉 │ 解釋更改原因

Conversation

1 茉莉為約翰・卡達和保羅・羅傑斯草擬了一個日程表。閱讀他們的對話，並且觀看短片，發生了甚麼問題？

Jasmine	... and I think that Diane can explain that later. Just a moment! ... Jasmine Goodman ... Oh, hello Diane ... yes, John and Paul are here already ... Oh dear! ... Right ...Yes ... . I'll tell them ... No, don't worry. Yes ... yes .... No problem ... OK ... Well, I hope she's better soon. ... Right, bye ... . Bye.
John	Is there a problem?
Jasmine	Yes, **I'm afraid there is.** That was Diane. Her daughter's sick.
Paul	Nothing serious, I hope?
Jasmine	No, I don't think so but she does need to take her to the doctor. **I truly apologize** but she can't come around the factory with you today. So **we need to adjust the schedule** because she really wants to do that with you.
John	OK.
Jasmine	So **I want to move forward** the visit to our test facility that we planned for tomorrow, to today ...
John	All right.

Jasmine	... and **move back** the visit to the factory to tomorrow so Diane can come as well. **She sends her apologies for changing the plan**.
Paul	No problem. And ... at dinner this evening? Will you come as well, or is it just Mr Harris?
Jasmine	Just Mr Harris. **I'd love to come but** unfortunately I have to babysit for a friend this evening. **I'm really sorry!**

Did you know?

英式英語用 *move* 或 *bring forward* 表示提早計劃做某事，而美式英語則用 *move up*。在英式英語裏，*move back* 和 *put back*，指推遲日子或時間做某事。

Understanding

DVD

2 再看短片一次，茉莉在日程表改了甚麼？

Today	Tomorrow
11.00 am – tour factory with Diane and Chris Fox	9.30 am – visit test facility. Meet Jim Gibson
1.00 pm – sandwiches in office	4.00 pm – taxi from Lowis Engineering to airport
3.00 pm – meet sales team	
6.00 pm – dinner with Diane and Mr Harris	7.00 pm – flight to Sydney

Key phrases

Apologizing	Changing arrangements
I'm afraid there's a problem.	*We need to adjust the schedule / change the plan.*
I truly apologize but	
She sends her apologies for	*I want to move / bring forward (UK) / move up (US)... . [←]*
I'd love to XYZ but	
I'm so sorry. / I'm so sorry for	*I want to move back / put back (UK) ... . [→]*

Practice

3 連接句子的兩部份。

1 They send their apologies   A up the meeting.
2 The boss wants to move   B but we're away on vacation.
3 I need to   C back the flight by two hours.
4 We'd love to   D for the delay.
5 The airline has put   E adjust the schedule.

4 將句中詞語排成正確順序。

1 sales team telephone want bring The conference call forward to the

_____.

2 I for hotel truly the problems with apologize the

_____.

3 I'm afternoon there's the change to a timetable afraid this

_____.

4 sent apologies his He for delay the

_____.

5 so presentation sorry we put I'm the to tomorrow back

_____.

5 從方框選取詞語完成句子。

truly   sorry   up   back   need   afraid

1 I'm _____ there's a problem with the flight.
2 I'm so _____ you had to wait.
3 I _____ apologize for the delay.
4 We _____ to change the schedule.
5 I'm moving _____ the meeting from 4 to 3.
6 I'm putting _____ the visit from 3 to 4.

Language tip

想別人明白某事非常重要，可以用助動詞 *do*，或用 *truly*、*really* 或 *so* 等表示強調。
She ***does*** need to take her to the doctor.
She ***really*** wants to do that with you.
I ***truly*** apologize.
I'm ***so*** sorry.

Speaking

6 你要打電話給公司的重要客戶沙地女士,告訴她四月七日發給她的日程需要更改。用以下的內容幫助自己。播放 Track 43 ,在嗶一聲之後講話,再聆聽 Track 44,對比你講的英語。

3–44
CD

Ms Sahdi's schedule, Tuesday – April 7
10.00 am – met by Mr King at the airport, show her the new office
11.00 am – meeting with Mr King and sales team
 1.00 pm – lunch in restaurant
 3.00 pm – visit factory and see new equipment
 7.00 pm – theatre and dinner

Ms Sahdi You need to make some changes to the schedule for tomorrow? No problem. Tell me.

You *(Apologize because Mr King is sick. You will pick her up from the airport.)*

Ms Sahdi I see.

You *(Bring forward the visit to the factory to 11 o'clock.)*

Ms Sahdi I see. After that?

You *(Apologize that you want to cancel lunch in a restaurant. Sandwiches in the office after the factory visit.)*

Ms Sahdi That's fine. I don't eat lunch normally. Any other changes?

You *(Move back the meeting with the sales team to 3 o'clock.)*

Ms Sahdi That's a good idea. And in the evening?

You *(Tell her you are taking her to the theatre and then to dinner.)*

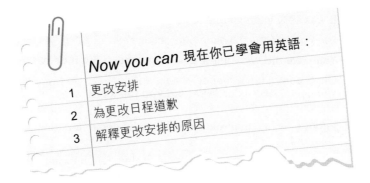

Now you can 現在你已學會用英語:

1 更改安排
2 為更改日程道歉
3 解釋更改安排的原因

22 How was your visit? 你的行程怎樣？

詢問過往的活動 ｜ 回答關於過去的提問 ｜ 詢問意見

Conversation

DVD

1 茉莉問約翰・卡達和保羅・羅傑斯他們昨天做了甚麼。閱讀他們的對話，並且觀看短片。保羅沒有看到甚麼？

Jasmine	... and Diane is just in a short meeting with Mr Harris. She'll be here in five minutes to go with us to the factory. But **how was** your visit to our test facility yesterday?
John	**It was** very interesting. We saw a lot.
Jasmine	**Did you** see the new computer centre?
Paul	**Yeah, we did**. Very impressive! **How much did it cost**?
Jasmine	Oh, **it cost** a lot of money! I'm sure Diane knows how much. You can ask her later. **What did you think** of the testing equipment for the pumps?
Paul	**I didn't** see it, I'm afraid. I stayed in the computer centre. But John did.
John	**I thought** it was fantastic. Very important for checking quality.
Jasmine	**How long did you** stay?
Paul	A couple of hours, I guess.

John	It was longer than that, Paul! We stayed at least three hours. And then your Managing Director, Mr Harris, met us and took us to dinner.
Jasmine	**Did you like** the restaurant?
Paul	Yeah, it was great.
Jasmine	How about you, John?
John	Yes, **I liked** it a lot. I can always eat Italian food.

Did you know?

英式英語和美式英語的拼寫有細微差異，例如 centre (英式) 和 center (美式)；color (美式) 和 colour (英式) 。

Understanding

DVD

2 再看短片一次，為每題選取最佳的答案 A、B 或 C。

1 John and Paul:

A are going to the test facility

B were at the test facility

C are at the test facility

2 Paul:

A tested the pumps

B thought about the testing equipment

C was in the computer centre

3 The restaurant was liked by:

A both of them

B only Paul

C only John

Key phrases

Asking opinions

How **was** your visit?	Did you **like** the ... ?
What **did** you **think** of ... ?	

Talking about the past

It **was**	I **didn't see** it. / I **thought** it was ... .
Did you **see** ...? → Yes, we **did**. / We **saw**	How long **did** you **stay**? → We **stayed** ... .
How much **did** it **cost**? → It **cost**	→ I **liked** it a lot / very much.

Practice

3 從方框選取詞語完成句子。

did	didn't	emailed	was	was	wasn't	were

1 I _____ speak to Mr Harris yesterday. He was sick.

2 Jasmine _____ him the report last week.

3 'How long _____ the flight yesterday?' 'It _____ that long. About two hours.'

4 _____ you see Diane this morning?

5 'How long _____ you in the meeting?' 'I think it _____ about three hours.'

4 將句中詞語排成正確順序。

1 How spend much did money you

_____?

2 night I the equipment checked last

_____.

3 you yesterday presentation email Paul Did the

_____?

4 did have Where lunch they

_____?

5 Fox did you Chris What show

_____?

5 用括號的動詞轉為一般過去式完成句子。

1 Jasmine _____ (meet) the visitors from reception at 9 o'clock.

2 Diane _____ (not go) to the test facility with John and Paul yesterday.

3 Jasmine _____ (email) the invitation to Mr Cao in March.

4 How long _____ (to be) your flight?

5 When _____ you _____ (check) the equipment?

6 _____ (to be) you at the airport on time?

7 Mr Harris _____ (to have) a meeting with Diane at 9 o'clock.

Language tip

談及在某時間發生，但已經結束的活動，會用一般過去式，例如：We stayed at least three hours. 或 It cost a lot of money.。
此外，想給意見時，可以在句首用 I think 或 I thought（如果説以前）。
參考 166 頁以更深入了解一般過去式，也可參考 170 頁，學習像 cost 等不規則動詞。

Speaking

5–46
CD

6 今天是星期五，你的經理想知道你這個星期做了甚麼工作。用以下的關鍵詞幫助自己回答他的提問。播放 Track 45，然後在吡一聲之後説話。聆聽 Track 46，對比你講的英語。

Manager	And can you tell me about this week? What did you do on Monday?
You	*(check / sales figures)*
Manager	I see. What about the sales presentation?
You	*(go / sales presentation / Wednesday)*
Manager	How was it?
You	*(think / excellent)*
Manager	Very good. And did you visit the customer afterwards?
You	*(visit / customer / Thursday)*
Manager	That's fine. Was Paul Rogers there?
You	*(Mr Rogers / not come / meeting)*
Manager	That's too bad.
You	*(What / you / do / this week?)*

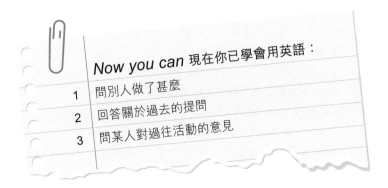

Now you can 現在你已學會用英語：

1 問別人做了甚麼
2 回答關於過去的提問
3 問某人對過往活動的意見

23 What can I do for you?
我能幫你做甚麼嗎？

請求協助 | 提供協助 | 接待訪客

Conversation

DVD

1 保羅需要茉莉幫助他，閱讀他們的對話，並且觀看短片。保羅請茉莉幫他做多少件事？

Paul	Jasmine, can you help me?
Jasmine	Yes, of course. **What can I do for you?**
Paul	I want to print the draft contract from this flash drive.
Jasmine	No problem. **Which document is it?**
Paul	There! The APU and Lowis Engineering contract document.
Jasmine	**Shall I** print one copy or two?
Paul	Er, two please, if that's all right.
Jasmine	Fine. **Would you like me to** staple them together?
Paul	Yeah. Thanks very much.
Jasmine	**There you are. Can I do anything else for you?**
Paul	No. That's all thanks.
Jasmine	Well, **let me know if you need something**.

Paul	All right. Thanks very much, Jasmine. Almost ready.
Jasmine	Ah, good. Thanks. Paul? John's downstairs when you're ready.
Paul	Great. Tell him I'll be with him in a moment.
Jasmine	Yeah. He'll be with him in a moment.

Understanding

)VD

2 再看短片一次，以下句子是正確 (T) 還是錯誤 (F)？

1 Paul wants Jasmine to print the final contract.　　　　　T / F
2 The contract is on Jasmine's computer.　　　　　　　　　T / F
3 Paul wants more than one copy of the contract.　　　　　T / F
4 Paul doesn't need any more help.　　　　　　　　　　　　T / F
5 John is waiting for Paul.　　　　　　　　　　　　　　　　T / F

Key phrases

Offering help

What can I do for you?	*There / Here you are.*
Which document / file / folder is it?	*Can I do anything else for you?*
Shall I … ?	*Let me know if you need something.*
Would you like me to … ?	

Practice

3 連接句子的兩部份。

1 Would you like　　　　　A　a car to the airport?
2 Can we do　　　　　　　B　he needs anything.
3 Let us know if　　　　　C　me to call a taxi?
4 Shall I book you　　　　 D　can I do for you?
5 What　　　　　　　　　 E　anything else for Ms Sahdi?

4 將句中詞語排成正確順序。

1 we for you arrange Shall a car rental

_____?

2 Cao like presentation Would else anything for Mr his

_____?

3 I do John Can anything else you, for

_____?

4 can do I for What them

_____?

5 Jasmine you something know if Let need

_____.

6 is Which it file

_____?

5 茉莉需要接待處莎莉的幫忙。將句子排成正確順序，然後聆聽 Track 47 核對答案。

1	Jasmine	Sally, can you help me with something?
	Sally	You're welcome!
	Sally	Sure. What can I do for you?
	Jasmine	Oh, a BMW I think.
	Jasmine	Good idea. Then she can get the keys from you.
	Jasmine	Yes. 9 o'clock is fine.
	Sally	OK. Well, which type of car does she want?
	Jasmine	No, that's all. Thanks a lot.
	Sally	All right, a BMW. Would you like me to ask them to deliver it to the company?
	Jasmine	I need to rent a car for Diane, but I haven't done it before.
	Sally	OK. Can I do anything else for you?
	Sally	No problem. Shall I order one for 9 o'clock?

Language tip

將某物遞給別人時，可以用 *There / Here you are*。

Speaking

48–49
CD

6 你的經理想你幫他處理關於出差的事，嘗試提出建議。播放 Track 48，在呸一聲之後說話，再聆聽 Track 49，對比你講的英語。

Manager	Can you help me?
You	*(Ask what he wants.)*
Manager	I need to fly to London on Thursday morning.
You	*(Offer to make a flight reservation for him.)*
Manager	Oh, thanks very much. And I need a hotel for Thursday and Friday.
You	*(Offer to reserve a room at the Anchor Hotel.)*
Manager	Yeah, that's a nice hotel.
You	*(Ask if he wants anything else.)*
Manager	No, that's all at the moment, thanks.
You	*(Tell him to ask if he needs anything else.)*

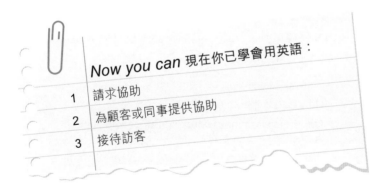

Now you can 現在你已學會用英語：

1 請求協助

2 為顧客或同事提供協助

3 接待訪客

24 Goodbye 道別

禮貌道別 | 感謝別人 | 祝旅途愉快

Conversation

DVD

1 茉莉正和約翰及保羅道別。閱讀他們的對話，並且觀看短片。為何星期五去機場有時比其他日子需要較長時間？

Jasmine	So, your taxi should be here soon.
John	How long is it from here to the airport?
Jasmine	Oh, only half an hour normally. But on Friday there's sometimes lots of traffic.
Paul	Well, our flight isn't until 7.00, so we have lots of time.
Jasmine	Oh, look, there's the taxi!
John	**Well, goodbye then,** Jasmine.
Jasmine	**Yes, goodbye. It was nice seeing you again**.
Paul	Yeah, and **thanks very much for** organizing everything for us.
Jasmine	My pleasure. **I hope you enjoyed your visit**.
John	Definitely. It was great visiting the factory and seeing the equipment in action.
Jasmine	**Good. I'm glad you enjoyed it**.

John	All right. We must go then.
Jasmine	Yes, the taxi's waiting.
Paul	**So, see you again soon, I hope.**
Jasmine	**Bye, bye. Take care.**
Paul	Thanks, Jasmine. **Bye.**
Jasmine	**Bye. Have a good flight!**

Did you know?

在英語裏，和重要的人道別時，會和上面的例子一樣，常常重複幾次。只説一聲 *Bye* 然後就走的做法不但不常見，而且還會顯得不友好。

Understanding

2 再看短片一次，為每題選取最佳的答案 A、B 或 C。

1 John and Paul's flight leaves:
   A before 7 o'clock in the evening
   B at 7 o'clock in the evening
   C after 7 o'clock in the evening

2 John was:
   A pleased with his visit
   B bored with his visit
   C disappointed with his visit

3 Jasmine says that she hopes John and Paul:
   A are very careful
   B come again soon
   C have a comfortable trip

Key phrases

Saying goodbye

Well, goodbye then.	*Good. I'm glad you enjoyed it.*
Yes, goodbye. It was nice seeing you again.	*So, see you again soon, I hope.*
Thanks very much for … .	*Bye, bye. Take care.*
I hope you enjoyed your visit.	*Bye. Have a good flight!*

Practice

3 將左邊的句子和右邊的回應配對。

1	I hope you enjoyed the presentation.	A	I hope so too.
2	Goodbye, take care!	B	My pleasure!
3	So, see you again soon I hope.	C	It was great.
4	Thanks very much for looking after us.	D	Thanks, bye.
5	Bye. Have a good trip.	E	Yeah, you too! Bye.

4 將句中詞語排列成正確順序。

1 Well, Chen goodbye, Mrs then

_____.

2 hope We you your enjoyed stay

_____.

3 glad interesting that your We're visit was

_____.

4 was again both great seeing It you

_____.

5 see hope you again So, soon, we

_____.

6 have flight Goodbye and a home good

_____!

5 寫出與每題底下回應相應的句子。

1 _____.

I hope to see you again soon too.

2 _____.

Definitely. It was a fantastic presentation.

3 _____.

I'm sure we will. Singapore Airlines is very good!

4 _____.

Yeah, thanks. Bye, Sally.

5 _____.

It was nice meeting you again too.

Language tip

感謝別人需要表現得充滿熱情，尤其是提起共同經歷的事時，可用以下形容詞修飾你對某事的看法：
It was great / fantastic / wonderful / terrific.

Speaking

6 你正在和公司的兩位訪客道別。播放 Track 50，然後在嗶一聲之後說話。用以下的關鍵字幫助自己，然後聆聽 Track 51，對比你講的英語。

50–51
CD

Visitor 1	Well, we must go. Goodbye then.
You	*(goodbye / nice / meet / again)*
Visitor 2	Yes, it was. And thanks for making the hotel reservation.
You	*(My pleasure / hope / enjoy / visit)*
Visitor 1	Oh yes, it was great. I learned a lot.
You	*(I / glad / visit / useful)*
Visitor 2	Definitely. So, see you again soon, I hope.
You	*(Yes / hope so / too / have / good / flight / goodbye)*
Visitor 1	Thanks. Bye.
Visitor 2	Bye bye.
You	*(goodbye)*

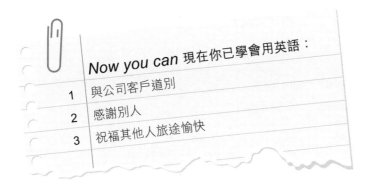

Now you can 現在你已學會用英語：

1 與公司客戶道別
2 感謝別人
3 祝福其他人旅途愉快

Unit 1   At reception 接待處

Conversation

1   John and Paul want to meet Diane Kennedy.

See page 6 for video script.

Understanding

2

1   False. They work at Australian Power Utilities.

2   True

3   True

4   False. They will only have to wait a moment.

Practice

3

1   Good evening, how can I help you?

2   Can I have your names, please?

3   Please could you complete these forms?

4   Someone will come down to get you.

5   Please have a seat.

4

1   B   2   D   3   A   4   C

5

Lowis Engineering – Visitor Form	
Surname / Last name	CARTER
First / Given name	John
Company address	Australian Power Utilities Inc, Block 7 Industrial Park, Canberra
Email	carter@apu.com
Visiting	DIANE KENNEDY
Time in 09:30	Time out _____
Signature *John Carter*	

6
Follow model in 5 above.

Speaking

7

Model conversation

You	*Good morning madam, can I help you?*
Guest	Yes, I have an appointment with Diane Kennedy for 11 o'clock.
You	*Can I have your name, please?*
Guest	Jane Taylor from Taylor and Curtiss Consultants.
You	*Right. Can you complete this security form, please?*
Guest	Can you give me a pen?
You	*Here you are.*
Guest	Thanks.
You	*Thank you. And could you wear this visitor badge, please?*
Guest	Of course.
You	*Please have a seat. Someone will come down to get you soon.*
Guest	Good! Thanks for your help!

Unit 2　Company visitors 公司訪客

Conversation

1　Diane Kennedy asked Jasmine to meet the guests.

See page 10 for video script.

Understanding

2

1　No, they don't.
2　Yes, she does.
3　Yes, they do.
4　Yes, she does.

Practice

3

1	C	2	D	3	E	4	F
5	A	6	B				

4

1　I'm John Carter / Paul Rogers and this is my colleague, Paul Rogers / John Carter.
2　We need to take the lift to the 3rd floor.
3　Excuse me, are you Mr Carter?
4　Come this way, please.
5　Mr Carter asked me to meet you.

5

Jasmine	(1) Excuse me, (2) are you Ms Ringwood?
Guest	Yes, that's right.
Jasmine	I'm Jasmine Goodman. (3) Diane Kennedy asked me to meet you.
Guest	Oh, hello Jasmine.
Jasmine	(4) Welcome to Lowis Engineering.
Guest	Thank you!

Jasmine	This way, please. We (5) need to take the lift to the 3rd floor.
Guest	OK.

Speaking

6

Model conversation

You	*Excuse me, are you Mr Stenson?*
Visitor	Yes, that's right.
You	*Hello. I'm Jan Smith. Mr Brown asked me to meet you. Welcome to our company.*
Visitor	Thank you very much.
You	*Come this way, please. We need to take the lift to the 8th floor.*
Visitor	Of course. This is a great building.
You	*Yes, it's a nice place to work.*

Unit 3   What do you do?
你做甚麼工作？

Conversation

1   Jasmine has to take the minutes in meetings.

See page 14 for video script.

Understanding

2

1   True
2   False. She usually stays in the office.
3   False. She takes the minutes.
4   True

Practice

3

1   D   2   E   3   C   4   F
5   B   6   A

4

1   E   2   D   3   A   4   C   5   B

5

Suggested answers

1   I'm a receptionist / an assistant.
2   I'm responsible for answering the phone.
3   I look after guests.
4   I reply to emails.
5   I deal with inquiries.

Speaking

6

Model conversation

Visitor	So, what do you do?
You	*I'm a sales and marketing assistant.*
Visitor	I see, that's interesting. Are you very busy?
You	*Really busy! The sales team travels a lot and I make all the flight and hotel reservations.*
Visitor	And are you responsible for anything?
You	*I deal with inquiries and send out information about our products.*
Visitor	Do you do anything else?
You	*Yes, I also help to organize the sales conference which is a big job!*

Unit 4 Making visitors feel welcome
令訪客覺得賓至如歸

Conversation

1   Jasmine calls Paul 'Mr Rogers' to be polite.

See pages 18–19 for video script.

Understanding

2

1   False. They have to wait for her to finish another meeting.
2   True
3   False. He wants some orange juice.
4   True
5   False. They say it's fine and tell Jasmine not to worry.

Practice

3

1   Would you like a cup of tea?
2   I'd like some coffee, please.
3   Would you like to sit down?
4   I'm sorry you have to wait.
5   Mr Carter should be here soon.
6   Would you like milk and sugar?
7   I'm afraid Mrs White is still in a meeting.
8   Here you are.

4

1   B   2   E   3   D   4   A   5   C

5

1   afraid, in
2   like, have / take
3   Here
4   take
5   some / a, please
6   should, soon

Speaking

6

Model conversation

You	Can I take your coats?
Visitor 1	Thank you.
Visitor 2	Here you are.
You	Would you like to sit down?
Visitor 1	Thanks.
You	Would you like some coffee or juice?
Visitor 1	I'd like some coffee, please.
You	What about you, Mr Carter?
Visitor 2	I'd like some orange juice.
You	I'm afraid Ms Kennedy is in a meeting.
Visitor 1	No problem.
You	She should be here soon.
Visitor 2	Thanks.

Unit 5   Small talk 閒聊

Conversation

1   Diane doesn't arrive for the meeting.

See pages 22–23 for video script.

Understanding

2

1   Frankfurt
2   Jasmine
3   No, they haven't.
4   Tickets for a football match.
5   In a French restaurant.

Practice

3

1	D	2	C	3	B	4	F
5	G	6	E	7	A		

4

1   Is this your first time here?
2   How's your hotel?
3   How was your flight?
4   Do you like the theatre?
5   Would you like to see 'The Lion King'?
6   How long are you staying here?

Speaking

5

Model conversation

You	How was your flight from London?
Visitor	Oh, not very good. The weather in London is terrible at the moment. It's nice to see some sunshine here.
You	Yes, it is. How is the hotel?
Visitor	It's very nice. Thank you for organizing it.
You	My pleasure. Is this your first time here?
Visitor	Yes, this is my first time. What should I do in the evening?
You	Do you like Spanish food?
Visitor	Very much!
You	Would you like to try a local restaurant this evening?
Visitor	Oh, yes! Very much. Thank you.
You	You're welcome. How long are you staying here?
Visitor	Until Friday. Then I fly back to London.
You	Well, I'll check where my boss is and tell him you're here.
Visitor	Thanks a lot.

Unit 6　Introductions 互相介紹

Conversation

1　Because she has already met them.

See page 26 for video script.

Understanding

2

1　False. They have never met Diane before.

2　True

3　True

4　True

Practice

3

1　Nice to meet you, John.

2　This is my colleague, Diane Kennedy.

3　Nice to meet you too.

4　I see you've met my manager, John Carter, already. / I see you've already met my manager, John Carter.

5　Pleased to meet you, Ms Goodman.

6　Please call me Jasmine.

4

1　I'm

2　already

3　is, colleague

4　too

5　like, introduce

6　call

5

[1]	Jasmine	Diane, can I introduce you to Mr Kline?
[2]	Diane	Nice to meet you, Mr Kline.
[3]	Mr Kline	Nice to meet you too. But please call me Mike.
[4]	Diane	Of course. And I'm Diane. Would you like to take a seat?
[5]	Mr Kline	Thank you.
[6]	Diane	And would you like some coffee?
[7]	Mr Kline	No, thanks.
[8]	Diane	So how was your flight?
[9]	Mr Kline	OK, but it was a bit late taking off.

Speaking

6

Model conversation

Colleague	So here we are! I'd like to introduce Lee Toms from DPU.
You	*Nice to meet you, Mr Toms.*
Lee	Nice to meet you too but please call me Lee.
You	*And I'm Sue. Please take a seat.*
Lee	Thank you.
You	*I'm sorry I'm late.*
Lee	No problem.
You	*Would you like some coffee?*
Lee	No, thanks.
You	*How was your journey here?*
Lee	It was fine. No problems.

Unit 7 An inquiry by email
用電郵查詢

Email

1 Jasmine is writing to Anchor Hotels.

Understanding

2

1 C   2 B   3 A

Practice

3

1 C   2 F   3 A   4 E

5 B   6 D

4

1 Please include your address and telephone number. *Or* Please include your telephone number and address.

2 We would like to invite you to a presentation.

3 I would be grateful if you could send us a brochure.

4 Please let me know if this time is possible for you.

5 I look forward to seeing you on Tuesday.

5

1 I **am** writing / **I'm** writing …

2 … is **organizing** …

3 We **would** like to …

4 … **let me** …

5 I **would** be grateful …

6 Please **include** a …

7 … to **hearing** from you.

Writing

6

Suggested answer

To Whom It May Concern (US English) / Dear Sir or Madam (UK English)

I am writing to ask about meeting facilities in your hotel.

On April 19, Crayton Car Rentals is organizing its Annual General Meeting for about 300 guests. Please let me know if your conference facilities are available on this date.

I would be grateful if you could send me information about room size, presentation equipment, catering facilities and costs.

I look forward to hearing from you.

Best regards (US) / Yours faithfully (UK)

Unit 8 A reply to an inquiry
回覆查詢

Email

1 A 25% discount on bookings before the end of February.

Understanding

2

1 False. The conference is for May 3.

2 False. The hotel also supplies a PDF file with information about the hotel.

3 True

4 False. They still have rooms available for May 3.

5 True

Practice

3

1 discount
2 email
3 price information
4 conference facilities
5 contact
6 available

4

1 If you would like further information, contact me on 0207 98 5151.
2 I am pleased to inform you that this date is available.
3 Thank you for your phone call this morning.
4 Please find attached our service information. / Please find our service information attached.
5 With reference to your email of March 27, ...

5

Dear Ms Goodman

Thank you for your phone call to my assistant this afternoon. [1]

With reference to the date of your event, we have rooms available at that time. [2]

Please find enclosed information about our conference equipment and prices. [3]

We are pleased to inform you that we have a special offer for catering facilities in May. [4]

If you would like further information, please let me know. [5]

Yours sincerely [6]

Priti Makesch

Writing

6

Audio script

Hi! This is Fran here. I'm in a meeting this afternoon. Can you answer the email from John Carter from Australian Power Utilities to say that if he wants to organize a meeting here on March 27th then it's ok? Send him also the price information for the meeting room and presentation equipment and tell him about the 5% discount on catering if he makes a reservation this week. He can call me tomorrow morning if he wants to speak to me. Thanks!

Suggested answer

Dear Mr Carter

With reference to your email this morning, we have a meeting room available on March 27. Please find enclosed price information for the meeting room and presentation equipment.

I am pleased to inform you that we have a 5% discount for catering if you make a reservation this week. If you would like further information, please contact Ms Stein tomorrow morning.

We look forward to hearing from you.

Yours sincerely

Unit 9 A follow-up email 跟進電郵

Email

1 She wants him to arrange three things.

Understanding

2

1 B
2 B
3 C
4 A
5 B

Practice

3

1 E
2 A
3 D
4 B
5 C

4

1 Are you able to come to the meeting tomorrow?
2 Would you mind sending a new contract as soon as possible?
3 Could you send the translation to Paul Rogers?
4 Would you be able to help me?
5 Can you finish the report by Friday?

5

Suggested answers

Could you _write the meeting report_?

Are you able to _go to the meeting on Friday_?

Would you mind _making the hotel / flight / restaurant reservation_?

Would you be able to _take my calls / my clients to lunch next week_?

Writing

6

1 help
2 show
3 able / available
4 mind
5 advise / let me know

Unit 10　A reply to a follow-up email
回覆跟進的電郵

Email

1 He makes six suggestions (including sending the photos in the post).

Understanding

2

1 Lunch.
2 A personal card.
3 Because the total price has changed.
4 The photos of the conference rooms.

Practice

3

1 Why don't you arrange a meeting?
2 Would you like me to send an email?
3 Have you tried moving offices?
4 What about changing the time of the meeting?
5 Let me know if you need another date.
6 Should I change the appointment?

4

Suggested answers

1 What about sending an email with the main points?
2 How about writing a brief summary report now?
3 If you like, I could *help you with the figures*.
4 Let me know if you need *any help with anything*.
5 Why don't you leave it until you get back?

5

1 some
2 Why
3 having
4 she
5 organizing
6 to check
7 need

Writing

6

Suggested answer

Dear Sally

Here are some ideas for the office party. Why don't we use the company cafeteria? It's very comfortable. What about starting at 6 pm and finishing at midnight? We need to work the next day!

For music, how about a live band? Would you like me to contact a friend of mine in the band, 'The Big Noise'?

Let me know if you need anything else.

Regards

[your name]

Unit 11   Invitations 邀請

Emails

1   A is formal, B is informal.

Understanding

2
1   True
2   False. It is for the afternoon and evening.
3   True
4   False. She also invites Paul.

Practice

3
1   It will be an opportunity for you to meet our Chairman.
2   We would like to invite you to a meeting on Thursday.
3   Would you like to come to lunch?
4   We hope you are able to attend the conference.
5   Are you free at 6 o'clock for a meeting?

4
1   Would you and Sally like to come to dinner on Saturday? / Are you and Sally free for dinner on Saturday?
2   I hope to see you then. / I hope you can come.
3   Best wishes

Writing

5
Suggested answer

Dear Mr Probst

I am writing on behalf of Ms Timms, Sales Director for CMCX Ltd. We would like to invite you to a meeting on Thursday April 7 from 10 to 12, followed by lunch at the Ritz Hotel. It will be an opportunity for you to meet Tim King, our Managing Director, and the sales team.

We hope you are able to attend the meeting and we look forward to meeting you on April 7.

Yours sincerely

[your full name]

Unit 12   Replies to invitations
回覆邀請

Emails

1   Mr Cao and Paul accept the invitation. Ms Schmidt and John cannot accept it.

Understanding

2

1   John
2   Mr Cao
3   Ms Schmidt
4   Paul

Practice

3

Thank you for your invitation to ... (F)

Thanks for the invitation to ... (I)

XYZ is pleased to accept your invitation (F)

XYZ is free and is looking forward to seeing .... (I)

Unfortunately XYZ is unable to attend ... due to ... (F)

I'm afraid I can't come because of .... (I)

We wish you success with your event. (F)

I hope everything goes well. (I)

4

1   attend
2   success
3   pleased
4   due
5   free
6   because of

5

1   Thank you for the invitation to the meeting on Friday.
2   We hope everything goes well on Friday.

3   Due to a business trip Ms Goodman is unable to attend.
4   Mr Rogers is pleased to accept your invitation.

6

Suggested answers

1   Thank you for the invitation to your sales conference on September 12.
2   My colleague Jasmine Goodman is pleased to accept.
3   We wish you success with your conference.
4   Yours sincerely

Writing

7

Suggested answers

Accepting the invitation

> Dear Ms Jones
>
> Thank you for your invitation to your company's 25th anniversary. I am pleased to accept your invitation and look forward to seeing you on July 4.
>
> Yours sincerely

Declining (= *not accepting*) the invitation

> Dear Ms Jones
>
> Thank you for your invitation to your company's 25th anniversary. Unfortunately, I am unable to attend due to another appointment.
>
> I wish you success with your event.
>
> Yours sincerely

Unit 13   Incoming calls 來電

Telephone calls

1

A Alan wants to speak to the Sales Department.

B Diane can't answer the phone because she is in a meeting.

Understanding

2

1 C   **2** B   **3** B   **4** A

Practice

3

1 C   **2** E   **3** G   **4** B
5 D   **6** A   **7** F

4

1 I'm sorry but Mr Carter's line is busy at the moment.

2 My boss will call back later.

3 I'm afraid he's on a business trip.

4 Can you call back tomorrow morning?

5 I'll put you through to the Sales Department.

5

Suggested answers

1 Can you call back later?

2 I'm afraid she's in a meeting.

3 Can you put me through to the Sales Department?

4 Can you hold, please?

5 I'm afraid she's still engaged.

Speaking

6

Model conversation

Customer	Can I speak to Mr Rogers, please?
You	*I'm afraid Mr Rogers is in a meeting.*
Customer	Oh, I see. Well, can I speak to Pauline Coates in the Sales Department?
You	*I'll put you through.*
Customer	Thanks.
You	*I'm sorry but Ms Coates' line is busy at the moment.*
Customer	Oh, I see.
You	*Can you hold?*
Customer	Hmm, I don't think so.
You	*Can you call back later?*
Customer	Yes, OK, thank you. Bye.
You	*Bye!*

Unit 14   Outgoing calls 打電話

Telephone calls

1 Jasmine only manages to speak to Andrea Schmidt.

Understanding

2

1 No

2 Jasmine wants to check the time of the meeting is OK for Ms Schmidt.

3 Mr Johansson is on a business trip.

Practice

3

1	C	2	A	3	F	4	E
5	B	6	D				

4

1 Can you put me through to James Harris, please?

2 I'm calling about the conference next month.

3 I just want to check your flight number.

4 Can you give me Mr Carter's mobile number?

5 Could I speak to Kate White, please?

6 Well, thanks very much Anthony.

5

[1]	Jasmine	Could I speak to Mr White, please?
[2]	Receptionist	I'll put you through.
[3]	White	Anton White.
[4]	Jasmine	Hi Mr White, this is Jasmine Goodman calling from Lowis Engineering.
[5]	White	Hello, Jasmine.
[6]	Jasmine	I'm just calling about the meeting next Tuesday at 10 o'clock. I just want to check if the time is OK for you.
[7]	White	The time is fine. No problem at all.
[8]	Jasmine	Oh good! Well, thanks a lot Mr White and see you next week.
[9]	White	See you then. Bye.
[10]	Jasmine	Bye.

Speaking

6

Model conversation

Receptionist	Apelles Hotels how can I help you?
You	*Hello this is Mary James from Capital Investments. Can you put me through to Cindy Fox?*
Receptionist	I'll put you through ...oh, I'm sorry she's on a business trip.
You	Oh, can you give me her mobile number, please?
Receptionist	Yes, of course. It's 0155 289 6645.
You	*That's 0155 289 6645. Well, many thanks. Goodbye.*
Receptionist	Goodbye.

Unit 15   When things go wrong
事情出錯時

Telephone calls

1

A   A wrong food order.

B   A delivery that has not arrived yet.

Understanding

2

1   False. She did order food from Benji's Catering.

2   True

3   True

4   False. She's waiting for a package she sent to Singapore to be delivered.

5   False. The package is still in Singapore.

6   True

Practice

3

1   D   2   A   3   E   4   B   5   C

4

1   Can you tell me when you will pick up the package?

2   It's concerning our order for office equipment.

3   Something is wrong with the package you delivered.

4   It's concerning my package, tracking number LO 743 KL.

5   What's happened to our delivery?

6   You sent the wrong delivery to our company.

5

Suggested answers

1   Can you tell me when the package will arrive?

2   Can you give me a refund?

3   Could you pick it up?

4   What's happened to our package?

5   You sent a wrong delivery.

Language tip

13 – 30	thirteen – thirty
14 – 40	fourteen – forty
15 – 50	fifteen – fifty
16 – 60	sixteen – sixty
17 – 70	seventeen – seventy
18 – 80	eighteen – eighty
19 – 90	nineteen – ninety

A H J K

B C D E G P T Z (US)

F L M N S X Z (UK)

I Y

O

Q U W

R

Speaking

6

Model conversation

Supplier	Jackson Office Supplies. How can I help you?
You	*This is Cathy King from Apcos Ltd. There's a problem with an order I made last week.*
Supplier	I'm sorry to hear that. Can you give me the order number?

You	*Yes, it's JYG 723 / 19 / BP. You sent the wrong ink for our printers.*
Supplier	Oh, I see.
You	*Could you pick it up and bring the right ink, TP2000?*
Supplier	No problem.
You	*Can you tell me when it'll be delivered?*
Supplier	I think tomorrow should be possible. Is that OK?
You	*That's OK. Thanks very much. Goodbye.*

Unit 16   Telephone messages
電話留言

Telephone calls

1   Diane is on holiday.

Understanding

2

1   He's flying to London, not Liverpool; next week, not next month.

2   Tina Jones, not James. Meeting on the 14th not the 4th.

3   Mark is emailing something to Diane not sending something in the post.

Practice

3

1   Can I leave a message for Mr Carter?

2   Would you like me to leave him a message?

3   I'll read the message back to you.

4   Could you take a message for Jasmine Goodman?

5   Can I just check the information?

6   Do you want to leave a message for Mr Rogers?

4

Audio script

Jasmine	Jasmine Goodman.
John	Good morning, Jasmine. It's John Carter here.
Jasmine	Hello John, how are you?
John	Fine thanks. Um … can I speak to Diane?
Jasmine	I'm afraid she's away this week. Would you like me to take a message? Or do you want to send her an email?
John	Actually, could you take a message? I'm driving to the airport at the moment.
Jasmine	No problem.
John	Can you tell her that I want to change the date of our meeting from the 13th to the 30th of this month if that's OK. And I've also changed the restaurant for our lunch. Tell her to meet me at The Anchor Hotel in Mayfair at 1 o'clock. I think she knows the place.
Jasmine	So, I'll read the information back to you: 'John would like to change the date of your meeting from the 13th to the 30th. Please meet him for lunch at The Anchor Hotel in Mayfair at 12 o'clock.'
John	No, 1 o'clock, not 12.
Jasmine	Oops, sorry! 1 o'clock ….

Telephone message

John Carter would like to change the date of your meeting from the 13th to the 30th. Please meet him for lunch at The Anchor Hotel in Mayfair at 1 o'clock.

Speaking

5

Model conversation

Customer	Can I speak to Mr Rogers, please?
You	*I'm afraid Mr Rogers is in a meeting.*
Customer	Oh, I see. I have some information for him.
You	*Do you want to leave a message for Mr Rogers?*
Customer	Um … yes, OK. Can you tell him that my conference in June is cancelled. If he wants to speak to me about it, he can call me on my new mobile. The number is 01521 300 9957.
You	*Can I just check the information? The conference in June is cancelled and Mr Rogers can call you on 01521 300 9957.*
Customer	That's right. Thanks very much. Goodbye.
You	*Goodbye.*

Unit 17 Conference arrangements
會議安排

1 The participants will eat lunch in the hotel restaurant.

2

1 True
2 True
3 False. She also wants a flipchart and four pinboards.
4 False. She arranges it for 4.30 pm.
5 True

3

1 projector   4 reserve
2 provide   5 forget
3 mind

4

1 Please could you reserve some tables for us?
2 I'd like to reserve some tickets.
3 Would you mind repeating that back to me, please?
4 Does the room have an Internet connection?
5 Can you organize a meeting for next week?

5

Audio script

Cindy	Apelles Hotel Reservation Department, Cindy Fox speaking. How can I help you?
John	Good morning. My name's John Pitt. I'd like to reserve a room for a meeting from 2 o'clock until 7 o'clock for October 19th.
Cindy	Are you a customer of ours already Mr Pitt?
John	Yes. It's Topaz Lighting.
Cindy	All right. How many participants will there be?
John	15.
Cindy	OK, let me check. Yes, that's fine, Mr Pitt. The Napoleon Suite is available.
John	Excellent, that's fine. Now, does the room include a multimedia projector?
Cindy	Yes, and Internet access. Is there anything else you need?
John	Could you provide a flipchart and DVD player?
Cindy	Yes.
John	Good. Now, can you arrange a coffee break for 4.30, please?
Cindy	OK. What about water and juice during the meeting?
John	Oh, good idea! Next, dinner: Would you reserve tables in the hotel restaurant for 7 o'clock?
Cindy	Certainly, Mr Pitt.
John	Good. Now, would you mind repeating that back to me?

Cindy	Of course. October 19th, the Napoleon Suite from 2 until 7 for 15 people. Dinner at seven and a coffee break at 4.30 plus water and juice in the meeting room. And you need a multimedia projector, flip chart and DVD player.
John	That's correct.

Customer name: John Pitt

Company: Topaz Lighting

Date: October 19

Time: 2-7 pm

Meeting room: Napoleon Suite

Participant numbers: 15

Equipment required: Multimedia projector, flip chart, DVD player

Refreshments: Coffee break + dinner in hotel restaurant, water and juice for the meeting

Time required: 4.30 coffee, 7.00 dinner

Cindy	All, right. For how many participants?
You	*For 14 participants.*
Cindy	Yes, that's fine. The Napoleon Suite is available.
You	*Does the room have an Internet connection?*
Cindy	Yes, it does. Is there anything else you need?
You	*Could you provide a multimedia projector and flip chart?*
Cindy	No problem. What about refreshments?
You	*Can you set up coffee and sandwiches for 12 o'clock, please?*
Cindy	Fine. I'll confirm this is in an email.
You	*Thanks very much. Bye.*

Speaking

6

Model conversation

Cindy	Apelles Hotel Reservation Department, Cindy Fox speaking. How can I help you?
You	*Hello, this is Jasmine Goodman. I'd like to reserve a meeting room for July 30th from 10 o'clock until 3 o'clock.*

Unit 18　Travel plans 旅遊計劃

Telephone calls

1 Diane will meet Mr Wasilewski on Wednesday afternoon.

Understanding

2

1　C　2　B　3　A

Practice

3

1　C　2　E　3　A　4　D　5　B

4

1 Does 10.30 work for you?
2 Would lunchtime be convenient for you Ms Kennedy?
3 Would it be possible for me to see him tomorrow?
4 Is John available on Monday morning?
5 Could you meet Jasmine at quarter to four?

5

[1]	Jasmine	… Diane will be flying to Warsaw on Monday. Do you have time on Monday?
[2]	Eva	On Monday? Hmm, that's difficult.
[3]	Jasmine	Well are you available on Monday evening? Ms Kennedy would like to take you to dinner.
[4]	Eva	That's very kind, but I have another appointment in the evening.
[5]	Jasmine	Mmm, well, would Tuesday morning be convenient for you?
[6]	Eva	Well after 10.00 perhaps.
[7]	Jasmine	Great! How about 11 o'clock? Does that work for you?
[8]	Eva	Sure. That would be fine.

Speaking

6

Model conversation

Customer	So you are flying to Madrid next week? Hmm, when can we meet?
You	*Would it be possible for me to see you on Tuesday?*
Customer	Tuesday? No sorry, I'm away on a business trip.
You	*Are you available on Wednesday morning?*
Customer	I'm afraid Wednesday morning is no good. I have to go to the doctor.
You	*Could you meet on Wednesday afternoon?*
Customer	Um … yes … I think so.
You	*Would 3 o'clock be convenient for you?*
Customer	Is a little later possible?
You	*I could meet at 4 o'clock at the latest because I have to leave by 6.00.*
Customer	Yes, that's fine. I'll see you then!

Unit 19 Welcome back 歡迎回來

Conversation

1 Paul bought Jasmine a present because she organized their visit to Lowis Engineering and booked them a hotel.

See pages 78–79 for video script.

Understanding

2

1 False. She comes down to meet them in reception.
2 True
3 False. Jasmine makes the hotel reservation for them.
4 True
5 True

Practice

3

1 D   2 C   3 B   4 A

4

1 That's really kind of you.
2 Nice to see you again too, Diane.
3 How are you. Tony?
4 Here's a small present from all of us.
5 Fine, thanks. And how about you?

5

1 to
2 too
3 are
4 thanks
5 well

6 for
7 My
8 this
9 is
10 at

Speaking

6

Model conversation

Colin	Hello! Good to see you again!
You	*Nice to see you again, too, Colin.*
Colin	How are you?
You	*Fine thanks, and you?*
Colin	Very well. And thank you so much for arranging my hotel room.
You	*You're welcome!*
Colin	And here is a small thank you present for all your hard work.
You	*Oh, that's really kind of you!*
Colin	My pleasure!

Unit 20   Plans 計劃

Conversation

1   John has already met Jim Gibson before.

See pages 82–83 for video script.

Understanding

2

Today

11.00 am – arrive Lowis Engineering

1.00 pm – tour factory with Diane and Chris Fox

3.00 pm – meet engineers

6.00 pm – dinner with Diane and Mr Harris

Tomorrow

9.30 am – visit test facility. Meet Jim Gibson

4.00 pm – taxi from Lowis Engineering to airport

7.00 pm – flight to Sydney

Practice

3

1	first	3	next	5	while
2	after	4	then	6	finally

4

1   Today I'm planning to listen to my English CD while driving to work.

2   First of all, we're having a meeting.

3   After that I'm having lunch with Jasmine.

4   Then I'm writing a report for my boss.

5   Finally, this evening I'm going to a movie.

5

Suggested answers

First of all, on Monday I'm flying to the US to visit our New York office.

After / After that, on Tuesday I'm meeting with the Sales Manager.

And then on Tuesday afternoon I'm having a tour of the warehouse.

Next, on Wednesday I'm having lunch with the Managing Director to discuss the business plan.

Finally, on Friday I'm doing some sightseeing and getting a flight back to London at 10 pm.

Speaking

6

Model conversation

Manager	Ah, there you are. Can you tell me about my schedule for tomorrow with Ms Sahdi?
You	*First of all, at 10 o'clock, you're picking up Ms Sahdi at the airport and showing her the new office.*
Manager	I see. What next?
You	*Next, at 11.00, you're having a meeting with Ms Sahdi and the sales team.*
Manager	Very well. And then?
You	*And then you're taking Ms Sahdi to lunch at 1.00.*
Manager	I see. After that?
You	*After that you're visiting the factory at 3.00 to see the new equipment.*
Manager	Good! Anything else?
You	*Finally, at 7 o'clock, you're going to the theatre and then having dinner.*

Unit 21   A change of plan 改變計劃

Conversation

1   Diane can't come in today because her daughter is sick.

See pages 86–87 for video script.

Understanding

2

Today

11.00 am – *arrive Lowis Engineering*
1.00 pm – *tour test facility*
3.00 pm – *meet Jim Gibson*
6.00 pm – *dinner with Mr Harris*

Tomorrow

9.30 am – *visit factory with Diane and Chris Fox*
4.00 pm – *taxi from Lowis Engineering to airport*
7.00 pm – *flight to Sydney*

Practice

3

1   D   2   A   3   E   4   B   5   C

4

1   The sales team want to bring forward the telephone conference.
2   I truly apologize for the problems with the hotel.
3   I'm afraid there is a change to the timetable this afternoon.
4   He sent his apologies for the delay.
5   I'm so sorry we put back the presentation to tomorrow.

5

1   afraid (sorry is also possible)
2   sorry
3   truly
4   need
5   up
6   back

Speaking

6

Model conversation

Ms Sahdi	You need to make some changes to the schedule for tomorrow? No problem. Tell me.
You	*I'm so sorry but Mr King is sick, so I'm picking you up at the airport.*
Ms Sahdi	I see.
You	*And I'm bringing forward the visit to the factory to 11 o'clock.*
Ms Sahdi	I see. After that?
You	*I truly apologize but I want to cancel the lunch in the restaurant at 1 o'clock and have sandwiches in the office instead.*
Ms Sahdi	That's fine. I don't eat lunch normally. Any other changes?
You	*I'm moving back the meeting with the sales team to 3 o'clock.*
Ms Sahdi	That's a good idea. And in the evening?
You	*I'm taking you to the theatre and then to dinner.*

Unit 22   How was your visit?
你的行程怎樣？

Conversation

1 Paul didn't see the testing equipment.

See pages 90–91 for video script.

Understanding

2

1 B   2 C   3 A

Practice

3

1 I <u>didn't</u> speak to Mr Harris yesterday. He was sick.
2 Jasmine <u>emailed</u> him the report last week.
3 'How long <u>was</u> the flight?' 'It <u>wasn't</u> that long. About two hours.'
4 <u>Did</u> you see Diane this morning?
5 'How long <u>were</u> you in the meeting?' 'I think it <u>was</u> about three hours.'

4

1 How much money did you spend?
2 I checked the equipment last night.
3 Did you email Paul the presentation yesterday?
4 Where did they have lunch?
5 What did Chris Fox show you?

5

1 met
2 did not / didn't go
3 emailed
4 was
5 did, check
6 Were
7 had

Speaking

6

Model conversation

Manager	And can you tell me about this week? What did you do on Monday?
You	*I checked the sales figures.*
Manager	I see. What about the sales presentation?
You	*I went to the sales presentation on Wednesday.*
Manager	How was it?
You	*I thought it was excellent.*
Manager	Very good. And did you visit the customer afterwards?
You	*I visited the customer on Thursday.*
Manager	That's fine. Was Paul Rogers there?
You	*Mr Rogers didn't come to the meeting.*
Manager	That's too bad.
You	*And what did you do this week?*

Unit 23　What can I do for you?
我能幫你做甚麼嗎？

Conversation

1　She does two things for him: prints the draft contract and staples the papers together.

See pages 94–95 for video script.

Understanding

2

1　True

2　False. It is on Paul's flash drive.

3　True

4　True

5　True

Practice

3

1　C　2　E　3　B　4　A　5　D

4

1　Shall we arrange a rental car for you?

2　Would Mr Cao like anything else for his presentation?

3　Can I do anything else for you, John?

4　What can I do for them?

5　Let Jasmine know if you need something.

6　Which file is it?

5

[1]	Jasmine	Sally, can you help me with something?
[2]	Sally	Sure. What can I do for you?
[3]	Jasmine	I need to rent a car for Diane, but I haven't done it before.
[4]	Sally	OK. Well, which type of car does she want?
[5]	Jasmine	Oh, a BMW I think.
[6]	Sally	No problem. Shall I order one for 9 o'clock?
[7]	Jasmine	Yes. 9 o'clock is fine.
[8]	Sally	All right, a BMW. Would you like me to ask them to deliver it to the company?
[9]	Jasmine	Good idea. Then she can get the keys from you.
[10]	Sally	OK. Can I do anything else for you?
[11]	Jasmine	No, that's all. Thanks a lot.
[12]	Sally	You're welcome!

Speaking

6

Model conversation

Manager	Can you help me?
You	*What can I do for you?*
Manager	I need to fly to London on Thursday morning.
You	*Would you like me to book you a flight?*
Manager	Oh, thanks very much. And I need a hotel for Thursday and Friday.
You	*Shall I reserve a room at the Anchor Hotel?*
Manager	Yeah, that's a nice hotel.
You	*Can I do anything else for you?*
Manager	No, that's all at the moment, thanks.
You	*Well, let me know if you need anything else.*

Unit 24   Goodbye 道別

1   There is more traffic on the roads on Fridays.

See pages 98–99 for video script.

2

1 B   **2** A   **3** C

3

1 C   **2** E   **3** A   **4** B   **5** D

4

1   Well, goodbye then, Mrs Chen.
2   We hope you enjoyed your stay.
3   We're glad that your visit was interesting.
4   It was great seeing you both again.
5   So, see you again soon, we hope.
6   Goodbye and have a good flight home!

5

1   See you again soon, I hope.
2   I hope you enjoyed the presentation.
3   Have a good flight!
4   Bye, take care!
5   It was nice meeting you again.

6

Model conversation

Visitor 1	Well, we must go. Goodbye then.
You	*Goodbye, it was nice meeting you again.*
Visitor 2	Yes, it was. And thanks for making the hotel reservation.
You	*My pleasure. I hope you enjoyed your visit.*
Visitor 1	Oh yes, it was great. I learned a lot.
You	*I'm glad you found your visit useful.*
Visitor 2	Definitely. So see you again soon, I hope.
You	*Yes, I hope so too. Have a good flight. Goodbye.*
Visitor 1	Thanks. Bye.
Visitor 2	Bye bye.
You	*Bye.*

1 At reception 接待處

莎莉： 早晨，請問有甚麼可以幫你？

約翰： 早晨，我們是來見黛安·甘迺迪的，約了十點鐘見面。

莎莉： 能請你們留下姓名嗎？

約翰： 可以，我們是澳洲電力公司的約翰·卡達和保羅·羅傑斯，這是我們的公司名片。

莎莉： 謝謝，我會打電話給甘迺迪女士。

保羅： 謝謝。

莎莉： 另外，能請你們填寫這份訪客保安表格嗎？

保羅： 當然可以。不好意思，可以給我一支筆嗎？

莎莉： 這是你要的筆。黛安？一位羅傑斯先生和一位卡達先生在接待處等你。沒錯，謝謝。

莎莉： 謝謝。能請你們戴上訪客證嗎？很快會有人下來接你們，請坐一下。

保羅： 謝謝。

約翰： 好的。

2 Company visitors 公司訪客

茉莉： 不好意思，請問你們是約翰·卡達和保羅·羅傑斯嗎？

約翰： 沒錯，我是約翰·卡達，而這位是我的同事，保羅·羅傑斯。

茉莉： 你好，我是茉莉·歌文。

約翰： 你好。

保羅： 你好。

茉莉： 黛安·甘迺迪叫我來和你們見面。歡迎來到洛維工程公司。

保羅： 謝謝。

約翰： 謝謝。

茉莉： 請到這邊來，我們要乘電梯，或者應該說，乘升降機到三樓。

保羅： 這幢大廈很不錯。

茉莉： 是的，在這裏工作很好。

3 What do you do? 你做甚麼工作？

約翰： 茉莉，你是做甚麼工作的？

茉莉： 啊，我是黛安的私人助理，因此我負責接電話和安排她的日程。

保羅： 她一定很忙吧？

茉莉： 對，她經常出差，機票和酒店全由我負責預訂。

約翰： 我明白。你有時會跟她一起去嗎？

茉莉： 不，甚少。我留在這裏，並負責辦公室的日常運作，解決任何會出現的問題。

保羅： 你要做的事情真多！

茉莉： 是，開會時，當然也是由我負責寫會議記錄。

保羅： ……而且你還要接待來公司的訪客。

茉莉：是，沒錯！啊，升降機到了，請你先進。

約翰：謝謝。

4 Making visitors feel welcome 令訪客覺得賓至如歸

茉莉： 我們到了。我可以幫你掛外套嗎？

約翰： 好的，謝謝。

茉莉： 請坐。抱歉，黛安還在開會，請問你想要一杯咖啡嗎？

約翰： 嗯……

茉莉： 還是一杯水或果汁？

約翰： 我想我還是要一杯咖啡，麻煩你。

茉莉： 要加奶和糖嗎？

約翰： 好的，麻煩你。奶和糖都要，謝謝。

茉莉： 羅傑斯先生，你呢？

保羅： 叫我保羅就可以了。麻煩你，我想要些橙汁。

茉莉： 保羅，這是你的飲料。

保羅： 謝謝。

茉莉： 不好意思讓你們等了那麼久，黛安很快會來。

約翰： 沒關係，請放心。

5 Small talk 閒聊

茉莉： 坐飛機還順利嗎？

約翰： 嗯，還好。但我們很早就要到法蘭克福機場辦理登機手續。

茉莉： 喔，是的，現在的機場保安檢查通常要花很長時間。住的酒店怎樣？

保羅： 很好，謝謝你幫我們預約。

茉莉： 能幫到你們是我的榮幸，這是你們第一次來這裏嗎？

約翰： 當然不是我們第一次來倫敦，但我們是第一次來你們公司。

保羅： 明白，而且我們對你公司的產品很感興趣。

茉莉： 那就好。你們會在倫敦逗留多久？

保羅： 一個星期。我們在週末可以做甚麼？

茉莉： 唔⋯⋯你喜歡足球嗎？你明白，不是説美式那種？

約翰： 是，非常喜歡。

茉莉： 那你們會想在週末去看車路士的球賽嗎？我可以幫你們訂票。

保羅： 謝謝，這真是個好主意！

約翰： 妙極了！

茉莉： 別客氣。此外，我為黛安和你們預訂了附近一家法國餐廳吃午飯，這樣可以嗎？

約翰： 非常好，謝謝！

保羅： 好極了。

茉莉： 好。我去看看黛安在哪裏，讓她知道你們來了。

保羅： 好。

6 Introductions 互相介紹

茉莉： 她來了！黛安，我向你介紹，他們是澳洲電力公司的約翰‧卡達和保羅‧羅傑斯。

黛安： 很高興認識你們。

約翰： 我也很高興認識你。甘迺迪女士，我是約翰‧卡達。

黛安： 叫我黛安就可以了。

約翰： 好，黛安。我是約翰，而這位是我的同事，保羅‧羅傑斯。

保羅： 黛安，很高興認識你。

黛安： 保羅，我也很高興能認識你。我想你已經見過我的助理茉莉了。很抱歉來遲了，我上一個會議延長了。

約翰： 不要緊，茉莉已好好招待我們。

黛安： 好，那請坐。

保羅： 謝謝。

7 An enquiry by email 用電郵查詢

寄件者：jasmine.goodman@lowis.com
收件者：info@anchorhotels.co.uk
日期：　2 月 7 日
主旨：　洛維工程公司的發佈會

致執事先生：

　我向貴公司寫信，目的是查詢倫敦酒店會議設施的資料。

　本公司，即洛維工程公司，打算於五月三 日舉辦一項活動，屆時將有五百個重要公司客戶出席。本公司希望可以於活動中，向客戶展示我們的器材和介紹產品。請讓我們知道是否可在當天預訂貴公司的會議設施。

　如貴公司能提供簡報設施、會議室大小及餐飲設施的資料，不勝感激。另外，請附上貴公司的聯絡電話和聯絡人名稱，以供洽談細節之用。

　靜候貴公司的回覆。

洛維工程公司

茉莉・歌文謹啟

8 A reply to an inquiry 回覆電郵查詢

寄件者：j.martin@anchorhotels.co.uk
收件者：jasmine.goodman@lowis.com
日期：　2 月 8 日
主旨：　回覆：洛維工程公司舉辦活動

歌文女士：

　感謝貴公司於 2 月 7 日發來的電郵。就貴公司對會議設施的查詢，請查收附件中的pdf 檔。以上資料也可於網頁 www.Anchorhotels.com 找到。

　此外，很高興通知您我們的優惠，在二月底前預訂的客戶都可享有 75 折優惠。而在 5月 3 日，貴公司會議當日，本公司有會議室可供預訂。

　如欲了解更多本公司服務的資料，請致電 020 8307 4001 聯絡本人。

安佳酒店

會議設施經理

莊・馬田謹啟

9 A follow-up email 跟進電郵

寄件者：jasmine.goodman@lowis.com
收件者：j.martin@anchorhotels.co.uk
日期： 3 月 20 日
主旨： 5 月 3 日洛維發佈會

莊先生：

你可以幫忙嗎？我公司的經理黛安・甘迺迪女士，希望來看你們酒店的會議設施，她想看酒店設施的情況，你能否在下星期安排這事？

第二，你可否為活動裏每位來賓準備禮物嗎？請問你能否為每位來賓準備一份不高於€50 的禮物嗎？

如果那沒問題，你可否將價錢總數列入新報價單內，然後發給我嗎？

非常感謝你的幫忙。順祝

一切安好

茉莉上

附註：我打不開你給我的會議室照片，請告訴我該怎樣做。

10 A reply to a follow-up email 回覆跟進的電郵

寄件者：j.martin@anchorhotels.co.uk
收件者：jasmine.goodman@lowis.com
日期：　3 月 21 日
主旨：　5 月 3 日洛維發佈會

歌文：

　　謝謝你的電郵和請求。我在你的提問之後寫上回覆：

1) 我公司的經理黛安・甘迺迪希望來看你們酒店的會議設施，你不介意安排這事吧？

一點也不介意。如果你想的話，我們可以帶甘迺迪女士參觀設施，並且招待她吃午飯。

2) 你能否為活動裏每位來賓準備一份禮物？

可以，沒問題。不如以你或甘迺迪女士的名義，附送一張心意卡給他們作為禮物？

3) 請問你能否為每位來賓準備一份不高於 €50 的禮物？

當然可以。你何不看一下附件的禮物清單，然後告訴我你認為最好的禮物。

4) 請問你可以將價錢總數列入新報價單內嗎？

可以。我還未完成新的報價單，但明天我會弄好它。請問你想我把報價單同時發給甘迺迪女士嗎？

5) 我打不開你給我的會議室照片。

你試過用 Microsoft PowerPoint 打開照片嗎？還是我應該將照片放在電郵內發給你？

　　我希望以上建議對你有幫助，如果你還需要其他東西，請告訴我。順祝

安好

莊上

11 Invitations 邀請

A

曹先生：

　　本人代表洛維工程公司的銷售總監黛安·甘迺迪女士寫信給您，誠邀您出席洛維發佈會，活動將於五月三日（星期四），下午十二時至六時在倫敦安佳酒店舉行，而當天晚上將有晚餐。

　　活動當天，本公司為主要客戶和合作伙伴展示我們的最新產品。屆時，您將有機會和本公司最頂尖的工程師和設計師見面交流。

　　請在附件查找是次活動的程序和場地。我們希望您能出席是次活動，期待您於五月三日蒞臨。

茉莉·歌文謹啟

B

約翰：

　　黛安叫我寫信給你。我們於五月三日會為主要客戶和合作伙伴在倫敦安佳酒店舉行洛維發佈會，展示我們最新的產品。活動會在中午開始，傍晚將設晚宴。你當天有空嗎？會否和保羅一起來？

　　當日的程序和舉行地點等詳細資料，已放在附件內，希望於五月三日與你們見面。

祝 一切順心

茉莉上

12 Replies to invitations 回覆邀請

A

> 歌文女士：
>
> 　感謝您邀請我們公司的曹經理出席洛維公司於五月三日的活動。曹先生樂意接受您的邀請，並將出席十二時至六時在安佳酒店舉行的晚宴。
>
> 張珍妮謹啟

B

> 歌文女士：
>
> 　關於您在三月七日發來的電郵，很可惜的是，舒默茲女士因要在當日出差，故無法出席洛維公司於五月三日的活動。
>
> 　祝願貴公司活動成功。
>
> 祝 一切順心
>
> 伊娃・菲力奇

C

> 你好，茉莉：
>
> 　感謝邀請我出席五月三日的活動。抱歉當天我將放假而無法出席。不過保羅當天有空，他期待能再與你和黛安見面。我希望你們一切順利。
>
> 祝 一切順心
>
> 約翰

Translation of conversations

13 Incoming calls 來電

A

莎莉： 洛維工程公司。我是莎莉·泰萊，請問有甚麼可以幫你？

艾倫： 你好，我是德州顧問公司的阿倫·傑伊。麻煩你，我想找你們銷售部的同事。

莎莉： 請等一等。我會將你的來電接駁給甘迺迪女士……你好，傑伊先生？很抱歉她正在通電話，請問你能等一下嗎？

艾倫： 呃，好，沒問題。

莎莉： 抱歉她仍在用電話，請問你能稍後再打電話來嗎？

艾倫： 嗯，好吧，再見。

莎莉： 再見。

B

茉莉： 這是黛安·甘迺迪女士的號碼，我是茉莉·歌文。

約翰： 茉莉，你好。我是澳洲電力公司的約翰·卡達。黛安在嗎？

茉莉： 噢，約翰，你好。很抱歉她現在不在，她在開會。

約翰： 我明白了，我今天要跟她談談。

茉莉： 她開會要到十一點鐘才完，你能晚一點再打電話來嗎？

約翰： 好，沒問題。我在十一點半再打來可以嗎？

茉莉： 好，可以。

約翰： 好，謝謝你，茉莉。再見。

茉莉： 再見，約翰。稍後再談。

14 Outgoing calls 打電話

A

茉莉： 啊，早晨。請問我可以和阿倫·傑伊談談嗎？……他正在開會，好，我將稍後再打電話來。……十二點鐘可以嗎？……好極了！請問你能把他的內線號碼給我嗎？……8-6-5-1。好，很感謝你的幫忙！

B

茉莉： 你好，麻煩你，我想和安瑞亞·舒默茲談談。……舒默茲女士，你好。我是洛維工程公司的茉莉·歌文。……我打電話來，是想談我們下星期三在倫敦的會議。我只想確認你可以出席。……好，非常感謝你，舒默茲女士。……下星期見，再見。

C

茉莉： 你好，我是洛維工程公司打電話來的，我叫茉莉·歌文。請問你可以幫我接線給約翰納遜先生嗎？……噢，在出差？……嗯……請問你可以把他的手機號碼給我嗎？……00 49 1552 8896441。此外，你能給我他的固網電話號碼嗎？……我知道了，他的號碼是00 49 899 315 96021。……好，很感謝你。

15　When things go wrong　事情出錯時

A

班治：　班治到會，請問有甚麼可以幫你？

茉莉：　有，我是洛維工程公司的茉莉‧歌文。我打來想問我今天下的訂單。

班治：　是？

茉莉：　我訂的十份特別行政午餐套餐有問題，你們送錯訂單了。

班治：　你們收到了甚麼？

茉莉：　讓我看一看送遞的單據。啊，對了，你們送了兒童派對特別套餐過來。

班治：　呃，我知道了。

茉莉：　你可以來我們的辦公室收回嗎？

班治：　好的，當然可以。

茉莉：　另外，請問可以退款嗎？我們現在真的不需要特別行政午餐套餐了。

B

TPS：　感謝你致電TPS。如果想安排取貨，請按1字。想查詢TPS運送包裹的最新情況，請按2字。

東尼：　早晨，TPS。我是東尼，請問有甚麼可以幫你？

茉莉：　噢，你好。我的名字是茉莉‧歌文。我想問關於我寄去新加坡的包裹。速遞好像出了問題，到現在還沒有送到。

東尼：　好，請問你可以給我貨運單的號碼嗎？

茉莉：　嗯……號碼是MU 76344 HJ。

東尼：　讓我幫你查一下……抱歉讓你等了那麼久，我恐怕這個包裹已經延誤，它現時正在新加坡的倉庫。很明顯送遞的地址出了問題。

茉莉：　真的嗎？它發生甚麼事了？

東尼：　房屋的門牌號碼似乎不存在，我可以和你確認嗎？是不是金果園路40號？

茉莉：　不是，是14！

東尼：　哦，是一四，我知道了。

茉莉：　你可以告訴我包裹甚麼時候會送到嗎？

東尼：　我們會將包裹搬上貨車，所以今天應該能送達。我誠心為造成的任何不便道歉。

Translation of conversations

16 Telephone messages 電話留言

A

茉莉： 茉莉•歌文。

阿倫： 早晨，茉莉。我是德州顧問公司的阿倫•傑伊。麻煩你，我想和黛安•甘迺迪通話。

茉莉： 很抱歉，她這個星期不在。傑伊先生，<u>可以幫你寫下留言嗎</u>？

阿倫： 好，可否幫我告訴她，我下星期飛往倫敦，將在銷售會議裏和她見面呢？

茉莉： <u>可否讓我確認一下</u>？你下星期來倫敦，而你將在銷售會議裏和她見面。

阿倫： 是的，沒錯。

B

茉莉： 你好，茉莉•歌文。

天娜： 茉莉你好，我是天娜•鍾斯。我可以和黛安説話嗎？

茉莉： 對不起，鍾斯女士，她不在這裏，她將在下星期一回來。

天娜： 好的，<u>你可否寫下我的留言</u>？

茉莉： 好的，當然可以。

天娜： 跟她説我在十四號那天來開會，而我的同事馬可•湯齊尼也會出席，不過我們十點鐘才到，我們從米蘭飛來要八點半才到。

茉莉： 好，<u>讓我覆述一次</u>：你和湯齊尼先生將從十點鐘開始出席十四號的會議，還有其他能幫你的地方嗎？

C

茉莉： 茉莉•歌文。

馬克： 你好，茉莉。我是馬克•保。

茉莉： 你好，馬克。

馬克： 黛安在辦公室嗎？

茉莉： 馬克，她這星期放假。<u>你想留言給她嗎</u>？

馬克： 你可以跟她説我打過電話來，但我也想給她發一封電郵。你可否把她的電郵地址給我？

茉莉： 當然可以。她的電郵是diane.kennedy@lowis-engineering.com。

馬克： <u>我讀一次給你聽</u>：diane一點 kennedy @ lowis連字符號 engineering一點 com。

茉莉： 沒錯，我會跟她説你打過電話來。

17 Conference arrangements 會議安排

仙迪： 阿柏納斯酒店訂房部，我是仙迪・霍斯，請問有甚麼可以幫你？

茉莉： 早安！我叫茉莉・歌文。我想預訂一個房間，用來在四月二十七日，即下星期五九點至六點鐘開會。

仙迪： 歌文女士，請問你們已經是我們的客戶嗎？

茉莉： 是，我們是洛維工程公司。

仙迪： 好的，請問參加會議的有多少人？

茉莉： 大約二十至二十五個人。

仙迪： 好，我查一查⋯⋯好了，歌文女士，拿破崙套房和威靈頓套房都可供預訂。

茉莉： 非常好，我想訂威靈頓套房，請問這間套房有投影機嗎？

仙迪： 有，而且可以上網，還有其他需要嗎？

茉莉： 請問你們可以提供一塊掛紙板和四塊佈告板嗎？

仙迪： 沒問題。

茉莉： 好，請問可否將休息時間設在十點十五分，而另一個休息時間設在四點三十分嗎？

仙迪： 好，請問需要在會議期間提供水和果汁嗎？

茉莉： 好主意！然後，午膳方面，請幫我在酒店餐廳訂一點鐘的座位。

仙迪： 沒問題，歌文女士。

茉莉： 好，能請你覆述一次嗎？

仙迪： 沒問題，二十七日星期五，在威靈頓套房九點至六點，有二十至二十五人。休息時間設在十點十五分，午餐時間是一點鐘，然後在四點三十分再設一個休息時間，並在會議廳提供水和果汁。

茉莉： 別忘了還有設備。

仙迪： 一部投影機，一塊掛紙板還有三塊佈告板。

茉莉： 不對，是一部投影機，一塊掛紙板，還有四塊佈告板。

仙迪： 抱歉，收到了。我會再發電郵給你確認。

茉莉： 謝謝，我的電郵地址是⋯⋯

18 Travel plans 旅遊計劃

茉莉： 黛安後天會飛往華沙，而下星期會來格但斯克。請問她那時有機會見到你嗎，華西維奇先生？

彼得： 嗯，我挺忙，但我確定我們能找到時間。

茉莉： 明白，你在星期二下午兩點鐘會有時間嗎？

彼得： 呃，恐怕沒有。我那天兩點至六點鐘有一個會議。

茉莉： 好，那星期三早上你方便嗎？

彼得： 啊，很抱歉，我當天九點鐘約了牙醫。請問甘迺迪女士在之後那一天有時間嗎？我指星期四。

茉莉： 對不起，她沒有時間。她在星期四中午之前要回到倫敦。請問你在星期三中午會有時間嗎？

彼得： 讓我看看，好的，我可以安排到。

茉莉： 好極了！那麼在兩點半你的辦公室裏與甘迺迪女士見面可以嗎？你看可行嗎？

彼得： 沒問題，我很期待能和她會面。

茉莉： 很感謝你，我會轉告她，再見。

彼得： 再見。

19　Welcome back　歡迎回來

茉莉： 茉莉‧歌文。你好，莎莉。……約翰‧卡達和保羅‧羅傑斯？好，沒問題。我去接他們。……好極了。莎莉，謝謝你。

保羅： 茉莉，很高興再次見到你！

茉莉： 你好，保羅。你好，約翰。我也很高興能再見到你們！

約翰： 茉莉，你好嗎？

茉莉： 我很好，謝謝你。你呢？

約翰： 非常好，謝謝。

茉莉： 你們辦理好入住酒店的手續了嗎？

約翰： 已經辦好了。

茉莉： 那就好。

保羅： 再次感謝你為我們準備的所有東西。

茉莉： 不用客氣。

保羅： 這是我們公司預備的一份小禮物，送給你聊表謝意。

茉莉： 噢！非常感謝你！你們真是太好了。

保羅： 不客氣。

茉莉： 我到樓上再打開它，準備好上樓嗎？

保羅： 好了。

20 Plans 計劃

茉莉: 這是接下來兩天的日程表,我可以向你們簡述一次嗎?

約翰: 好,當然可以。

茉莉: 好。首先,這個下午你們會和黛安一起見工廠經理克里斯·霍士,他們想帶你們到工廠參觀。

保羅: 很好。

茉莉: 在克里斯帶你們參觀之後,黛安想給你們看看我們新器材的意念,你們也可以和我們的工程師説話。接着,黛安會帶你們去吃晚飯,我們公司的營運總監哈維斯先生也會同行。

約翰: 聽起來不錯。

茉莉: 然後,明天早上九點半時,我和黛安會從酒店駕車接你們,到我們在倫敦外圍的測試設施,你們可以看到我們的設備運作的情況。

保羅: 應該會很有趣。

茉莉: 希望如此。當你們在那裏的時候,你們可以見到測試經理占·吉普森,他會帶你們看所有東西。

約翰: 好,其實我已經認識占。

茉莉: 啊,那就好。最後,大約四點左右會有的士從這裏接你們去機場。你們回澳州的飛機應該是在七點。

保羅: 是的,沒錯。整個日程聽起來很有條理,茉莉,再次感謝你的幫忙。

茉莉: 不用客氣。

21 A change of plan 改變計劃

茉莉: ⋯⋯我想黛安可以之後再解釋。請稍等!⋯⋯茉莉·歌文⋯⋯嗯,你好,黛安,⋯⋯是的,約翰和保羅已經來了⋯⋯噢!⋯⋯對⋯⋯是⋯⋯。我會跟他們説的⋯⋯不,不用擔心。是⋯⋯是的⋯⋯沒問題⋯⋯好⋯⋯我希望她盡快康復⋯⋯好,再見⋯⋯再見。

約翰: 有問題嗎?

茉莉: 恐怕有,黛安那邊出了問題,她女兒病了。

保羅: 我希望不是甚麼嚴重的病?

茉莉: 不是,我不認為是嚴重的病,但黛安要帶她女兒去看醫生。我衷心向你們道歉,她今天不能陪你們去工廠了。我們需要更改日程,因為她真的很想和你們一起去。

約翰: 好的。

茉莉: 那麼我提早日程,將明天參觀測試設施的計劃改成今天⋯⋯

約翰: 沒問題。

茉莉： ……然後<u>推遲參觀工廠的計劃</u>，改至明天，讓黛安也可以來。<u>她為改變計劃的事致歉</u>。

約翰： 沒關係 。 然後……今晚吃晚飯，你會來嗎？還是只有哈維斯先生來？

茉莉： 只有哈維斯先生會來，<u>我很想來</u>，<u>但我晚上要幫朋友照顧小孩。非常抱歉</u>！

22 How was your visit? 你的行程怎樣？

茉莉： ……黛安正和哈維斯先生開一個簡短會議。她五分鐘後會來和我們一起到工廠。你們昨天參觀了測試設施，<u>覺得怎樣</u>？

約翰： <u>昨天的參觀非常有趣</u>，我們看到很多東西。

茉莉： 你們<u>有沒有</u>看新的電腦中心嗎？

保羅： <u>我們有</u>，太了不起了！興建這個中心<u>花了多少錢</u>？

茉莉： 嗯，<u>花了很多錢</u>。我肯定黛安會知道花了多少，你之後可以問她。<u>你覺得泵的測試設備怎樣</u>？

保羅： 恐怕<u>我沒有</u>看到，我昨天留在電腦中心裏面，但約翰看到。

約翰： <u>我認為那些</u>設備妙極了，對檢查品質非常重要。

茉莉： <u>你們留了多久</u>？

保羅： 我想大約幾個小時吧。

約翰： 比幾個小時更多吧，保羅。我們逗留了起碼三個小時。然後你們的營運董事哈維斯先生和我們見面，並帶我們吃晚餐。

茉莉： <u>你們喜歡那間餐廳嗎</u>？

保羅： 那間餐廳非常好。

茉莉： 約翰，你呢？

約翰： <u>我很喜歡那間餐廳</u>。我很喜歡吃意大利菜，常常吃也可以。

23 What can I do for you? 我能幫你做甚麼嗎？

保羅： 茉莉，你可以幫我嗎？

茉莉： 好，當然可以，<u>我能幫你做甚麼</u>？

保羅： 我要把USB記憶棒裏的合約草稿打印出來。

茉莉： 沒問題。<u>是哪份文件</u>？

保羅： 在這裏，澳州電力公司和洛維工程公司的合約文件。

茉莉： <u>我應該</u>印一份還是兩份？

保羅： 嗯，如果可以的話，印兩份吧，麻煩你。

茉莉： 沒問題，<u>你想我</u>把這兩份釘起來<u>嗎</u>？

保羅： 對，謝謝你。

茉莉： 釘好了，<u>給你</u>。還能幫你做甚麼嗎？

保羅： 沒有，就這些了，謝謝你。

茉莉： <u>如果你還需要甚麼，請告訴我。</u>

保羅： 好的。茉莉，謝謝你，快可以了。

茉莉： 好，謝謝。保羅？約翰在樓下等你。

保羅： 非常好，告訴他我很快會來。

茉莉： 是的，他很快會和他一起。

24 Goodbye 道別

茉莉： 你們的的士應該很快會到。

約翰： 這裏去機場要多長時間？

茉莉： 一般只需要半個小時，但在星期五有時會交通擠塞。

保羅： 我們的飛機七點鐘才起飛，所以我們時間很多。

茉莉： 噢！看，的士來了！

約翰： 茉莉，<u>那麼再見了。</u>

茉莉： 是的，<u>再見了</u>。很高興可以再次見到你們。

保羅： 是的，<u>很感謝你為我們安排一切。</u>

茉莉： 我很樂意效勞。<u>希望你享受這次的行程。</u>

約翰： 當然了，能去工廠參觀和看到機器運作真是太好了。

茉莉： <u>那就好</u>，<u>很高興你享受這些。</u>

約翰： 好了，我們要走了。

茉莉： 對，的士在等。

保羅： <u>希望在不久的將來能再和你見面。</u>

茉莉： <u>再見</u>，<u>保重。</u>

保羅： 茉莉，謝謝，再見。

茉莉： <u>再見</u>，<u>祝旅途愉快。</u>

Key phrases for speaking

Dealing with visitors at reception 在接待處接待訪客

Good morning / afternoon / evening. 早晨 / 午安 / 傍晚好
How can I help you? 請問有甚麼可以幫你？
Can I have your names, please? 能否請你留下姓名？
I'll call Mr / Mrs / Ms … . 我會打電話給……先生 / 太太 / 女士。
Can you complete this form, please? 能否請你填寫這份表格？
Could you wear this badge, please? 能否請你戴上這個訪客證？
Please take a seat. 請坐。
Someone will come down to get you. 有人下來接你們。

Meeting company guests 與公司的訪客見面

Excuse me, are you … ? 不好意思，你是……嗎？
I'm … . 我是……。
This is my colleague. … . 這是我的同事。
… asked me to meet you. ……叫我來和你們見面。
Welcome to … . 歡迎來到……。
We need to take the lift / stairs to the 2nd floor. 我們要乘電梯 / 爬樓梯上三樓（美式英語）/ 上二樓（英式英語）。
Come this way, please. 請來這邊。
After you. 你先請。

Asking about and describing responsibilities 詢問和描述工作內容

What do you do? 你是做甚麼工作的？
Is he / she busy? / Are you busy? 他 / 她 / 你是不是經常都很忙？
Do you travel with him / her? 你會和他 / 她一起出差嗎？
I'm a team assistant / PA / receptionist. 我是一名團隊助理 / 私人助理 / 接待員。
I work … . 我做……。
I make sure that … . 我確保……。
I book (hotels / tickets / flights). 我預訂酒店 / 機票 / 航班。
I answer the phone. 我接聽電話。
I reply to emails. 我回覆電郵。
I'm responsible for … . 我負責……。
I deal with … . 我處理……。

Polite offers and apologies 有禮貌地招待別人和表示抱歉

Can I take your coats? 我可以幫你掛外套嗎？
Would you like to sit down / have a seat? 請坐。
Would you like some / a cup of coffee? 你想要些 / 一杯咖啡嗎？
Would you like milk and sugar? 要加奶和糖嗎？
What about you …? 那你呢……？
Here you are. 這是給你的。
I'm sorry you have to wait, but … should be here soon. 我很抱歉要你等那麼久，但……該很快來。
I'm afraid that … is (still) in a meeting. 抱歉，……（還）在開會。

Making small talk 閒聊

How was your flight / trip / journey? 你的航班 / 行程 / 旅途順利嗎？
How is the hotel? 酒店怎樣？
Is this your first time here? 這是你第一次來嗎？
How long are you staying in ...? 你們會在⋯⋯逗留多久？
What should we do ...? 我們該做甚麼⋯⋯？
Do you like (the city)? 你喜歡⋯⋯ [那城市] 嗎？
Would you like to (sit down)? 你會想⋯⋯坐一下嗎？

Introducing other people 介紹其他人

I'd like to introduce ... from ...? 我向你介紹，這是來自⋯⋯的⋯⋯。
Nice to meet you. 很高興認識你。
Nice to meet you, too. 我也很高興認識你。
Please, call me ... . 請稱呼我⋯⋯就可以了。
This is my colleague ... . 這是我的同事⋯⋯。
Pleased to meet you. 很高興認識你。
Pleased to meet you, too. 我也很高興認識你。
I see you've met ... already. 我想你已經見過⋯⋯了。

Dealing with incoming phone calls 處理來電

Please hold. 請稍等。
I'll put you through to ... . 我會幫你接駁給⋯⋯。
I'm sorry but her line's busy at the moment. 很抱歉，但她現時正在通電話。
Can you hold? 你可以等一下嗎？
I'm afraid the line's still engaged (UK). / She's / He's still on the line (US). 我恐怕還是在佔線 / 她 / 他仍然在通電話。
Can you call back later? 你能晚一點再打電話來嗎？
I'm afraid she's not available at the moment. 我恐怕她現在不能接聽你的電話。
I'll call back at ... . 我會在⋯⋯時再打過來。
(Maybe) speak to you later. 稍後再談。

Making phone calls 打電話

This is ... calling from ... . 這是⋯⋯，從⋯⋯打電話來。
Could I speak to ... , please? 請問我可以和⋯⋯談嗎？
Can you put me through to ... , please? 你能幫我接線給⋯⋯嗎？
Hello, I'd like to speak to ... , please. 你好，麻煩你，我想和⋯⋯談。
Can you give me his extension number, please? 請問你能把他的內線號碼給我嗎？
I'm calling about ... . 我打電話來是想說⋯⋯。
I just want to check ... . 我只想確認⋯⋯。

Describing problems and asking for information 描述問題和查詢資料

There's a problem with ... . ⋯⋯有問題。
It's concerning ... . 有關⋯⋯。
You sent the wrong / a faulty delivery / order. 你送錯訂單了。
Something's gone wrong with ... . ⋯⋯出了問題。
Could you collect it / pick it up? 你可以來⋯⋯拿走 / 收回嗎？

Key phrases for speaking

Can you give us a refund? 請問可以讓我們退款嗎？
What's happened to …? ……發生了甚麼事？
Can you tell me when it'll be delivered? 你可以告訴我包裹在甚麼時候會送到？

Taking and leaving a phone message 寫下留言或給別人留言

Can I take a message? 可否幫你寫下留言？
Do you want to leave a message for her? 你想留言給她嗎？
Could you take a message? 你可以寫下我的留言嗎？
Can I just check that? 可否讓我確認一下？
Let me repeat that: … . 讓我覆述一次：……。
I'll read that back to you: … . 我將重複讀一次給你聽：……。

Making a reservation for a meeting room 預訂會議室

I'd like to book a room for a … . 我想為……訂一個房間。
Does the room have a …? 這個房間有……嗎？
Could you provide a … and …? 可否提供……和……嗎？
Can you organize / set up a (coffee break) for …? 可否將休息時間設在……？
Please could you reserve / book tables in the hotel restaurant? 請問你能否幫我在酒店餐廳訂位嗎？
Would you mind repeating that back to me? 能請你覆述一次給我聽嗎？
Don't forget the … . 別忘了那個……

Asking for an appointment 預約時間

Would it be possible for her to see you then / on (*Monday*) / at (*2 o'clock*)? 她能在那時 / 星期一 / 兩點鐘……有可能見你嗎？
Do you have time on (*Friday*)? 你在星期五會有時間嗎？
Would (*Monday*) be convenient for you? 星期一你會方便嗎？
Are you / Is she available on (*Thursday*)? 請問你 / 她星期四有空嗎？
Could you meet (*Diane*) at (*4.30*)? 可否在四點半與黛安見面？
Does that work for you? 你看那樣可行嗎？

Greeting people you know, giving and receiving a gift 問候認識的人、送禮物和收禮物

Good to see you again. 很高興再次見到你！
Nice to see you again, too! 我也很高興能再見你！
How are you? 你好嗎？
Fine thanks. And you? / How about you? 我很好，謝謝。你呢？
Very well, thanks. 非常好，謝謝。
This is a small present from … . 這是……預備的一份小禮物。
Thank you very much! That's really kind of you. 非常感謝你！你們真是太好了！

Outlining a schedule 概述日程表

First of all, … . 首先，……。
After / After that, … . 之後，……。
And then … . 然後，……。
Next … . 接着，……。
While … . 當……。
Finally, … . 最後，……。

Apologizing 道歉

I'm afraid there's a problem. 恐怕有問題。
I truly apologize but … . 我衷心道歉，但是……。
She sends her apologies for … . 她對……致歉。
I'd love to … but … . 我很想……但……。
I'm so sorry. / I'm so sorry for (*the mix-up / the inconvenience*). 我非常抱歉 / 我為混亂 / 不便致歉。

Changing arrangements 更改安排

We need to adjust the schedule / change the plan. 我們要調整日程 / 更改計劃。
I want to bring forward (UK) / move up (US) … . 我要提早……。
I want to move / put back … . 我要推遲……。

Asking opinions 詢問意見

How was your visit? 你的行程怎樣了？
What did you think of …? 你覺得……怎樣？
Did you like the …? 你喜歡……嗎？

Talking about the past 談過往的活動

It was … . 那個……。
Did you see …? → Yes, we did. / We saw … . 你有沒有看到？→ 我們有。/ 我們看到……。
How much did it cost? → It cost …. 那個花了多少錢？→ 花了……。
I thought it was … . / I didn't see it. 我想過那是……。/ 我沒有看到。
How long did you stay? → We stayed … . 你們逗留了多久？→ 我們逗留了……。
I liked it. 我喜歡它。

Offering help 提供協助

What can I do for you? 我能幫你做甚麼？
Which document / file / folder is it? 是哪份文件 / 哪個檔案 / 哪個文件夾？
Shall I …? 我應該……嗎？
Would you like me to …? 你想我……嗎？
There / Here you are. 給你。
Can I do anything else for you? 我還能幫你做甚麼嗎？
Let me know if you need anything. 如果你還需要甚麼，請告訴我。

Saying goodbye 道別

Well, goodbye then. 那麼再見了。
Yes, goodbye. It was nice seeing you again. 是的，再見了。很高興可以再次見到你們。
Thanks very much for … . 很感謝……。
I hope you enjoyed your visit. 我希望你享受這次行程。
Good. I'm glad it was useful. 好，我很高興那是有用的。
So, see you again soon, I hope. 希望在不久的將來能再和你見面。
Bye, bye. Take care. 再見，保重。
Bye. Have a good flight! 再見，祝旅途愉快。

Key phrases for writing

Asking for information 查詢資料

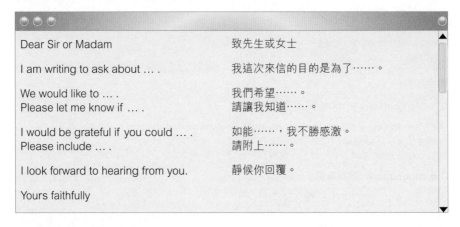

Dear Sir or Madam	致先生或女士
I am writing to ask about … .	我這次來信的目的是為了⋯⋯。
We would like to … .	我們希望⋯⋯。
Please let me know if … .	請讓我知道⋯⋯。
I would be grateful if you could … .	如能⋯⋯，我不勝感激。
Please include … .	請附上⋯⋯。
I look forward to hearing from you.	靜候你回覆。
Yours faithfully	

Giving information 提供資料

Dear Mr / Mrs / Ms … 致先生 / 太太 / 女士⋯⋯

Thank you for your email of … . / With reference to your request … , please find attached … .
感謝您於⋯⋯的電郵。就有關你的⋯⋯請查收附件的⋯⋯我很高興能通知您⋯⋯。

I am pleased to inform you … . 我很高興能通知您⋯⋯。

If you would like further information … , please contact me on … .
如欲了解更多有關⋯⋯的資料。請聯絡本人⋯⋯。

Yours sincerely

Asking for help 請求協助

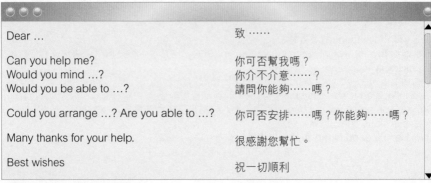

Dear …	致 ⋯⋯
Can you help me?	你可否幫我嗎？
Would you mind …?	你介不介意⋯⋯？
Would you be able to …?	請問你能夠⋯⋯嗎？
Could you arrange …? Are you able to …?	你可否安排⋯⋯嗎？你能夠⋯⋯嗎？
Many thanks for your help.	很感謝您幫忙。
Best wishes	祝一切順利

Making suggestions and offering help 提出建議和提供協助

Dear Sir or Madam	致先生或女士
What / How about +ing ...?	不如……好嗎？
Why don't I ...?	我何不……？
Why don't you ...?	你何不……？
Have you tried ...?	你曾經嘗試過……嗎？
If you like, we could	如果你想，我們可以……
Would you like me to ...?	請問你想我……嗎？
Should I ...?	我應該……嗎？
Let me know if you need anything else.	如果你還需要其他東西，請告訴我。
Kind regards	謹致問候

Key phrases for writing

Invitations 邀請

Formal 正式

Dear ...

I am writing on behalf of ... . We would like to invite you to ... . 本人代表……給您寫信。我們想邀請您……

It will be an opportunity for you ... . 這是個很好的機會……

Please find attached (*directions to our office*). 請見附件（往本公司的路線資料）

We hope you are able to attend and we look forward to meeting you on ... . 敬希參加。期待在……與您會面。

Yours sincerely 敬上 / 謹啟

Informal 非正式

Dear ...

... asked me to write to you. On (*month / day*) we are organizing ... . ……請我給您寫信。（月/日）我們將舉辦……

Are you free on this date, and would you like to come? 您是否有空出席此活動？

The agenda for the day and the location details are attached. I hope to see you on May 3. 節目流程及活動地點的詳細資料已列於附件。期待在五月三日與您見面。

Best wishes 祝一切順利

Replying to invitations 回應邀請

Formal 正式

Dear ...

Thank you for your invitation to ... on (*month / day*). ... is pleased to accept your invitation and will attend. 謝謝您邀請本人（月／日）到……。……非常樂意接受邀請及出席是次活動。

Yours sincerely 敬上／謹啟

Dear ...

With reference to your email of (*month / day*), unfortunately ... is unable to attend due to ... . 關於您（月／日）的電郵，本人因……未能出席是次活動。

We wish you success for your event. 我們預祝貴公司之活動順利舉行。

Best regards 祝一切安好

Hi Jasmine

Thanks for the invitation to the event on (*month / day*). I'm afraid I can't come because ... . But ... is free and he's looking forward to seeing you again. I hope everything goes well. 謝謝您邀請我參加（月／日）的活動。因……，抱歉未能參與此活動。然而，……有空出席此活動，而他非常期待與您再次見面。祝一切順利。

Regards 祝好

在英國，信封標準地址的寫法是：

Mr / Mrs / Ms A Brown	收信人名稱
Lowis Engineering PLC	收信人的公司 / 組織名稱
Lowis House	建築物的名稱 (如適用)
21 Wardour Street	建築物的號碼和街名
London	市 / 鎮
W1 0TH	郵政編號
United Kingdom	國家

在美國，信封標準地址的寫法是：

Jonathan Brown	收信人名稱
Lowis Engineering	收信人的公司 / 組織名稱
10 East 53rd Street	建築物的號碼和街名
New York NY 10022	城市、州份、郵政區號

但有些國家的做法並不相同。例如，在日本，收信人名稱會放在地址最下面。而在法國，除了收信人名稱外，全個地址的字母都要大寫。可使用互聯網查詢不同國家的地址寫法。

Email signatures 電郵簽名

有些公司有標準的電郵簽名，以下是茉莉的電郵簽名：

Jasmine Goodman ■ Personal Assistant to Diane Kennedy
Lowis Engineering PLC, 21 Wardour St, London W1 0TH
Tel. no. +44 (0)20 8307 4001 ■ Fax no. +44 (0)20 8307 4001

Out-of-office messages 出差通知

要通知別人自己出差，可參考以下電郵：

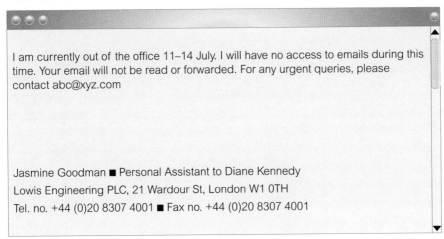

I am currently out of the office 11–14 July. I will have no access to emails during this time. Your email will not be read or forwarded. For any urgent queries, please contact abc@xyz.com

Jasmine Goodman ■ Personal Assistant to Diane Kennedy
Lowis Engineering PLC, 21 Wardour St, London W1 0TH
Tel. no. +44 (0)20 8307 4001 ■ Fax no. +44 (0)20 8307 4001

Lowis Engineering

Schedule:

John Carter and Paul Rogers, Australian Power Utilities

Tuesday 15th November

1.30–3.30	Tour of factory
	with Chris Fox (Factory Manager) and Diane Kennedy
3.30–5.00	Discussion of ideas for new equipment
	with Diane Kennedy and the team of engineers
6.30 onwards	Dinner
	with Mr Harris (Managing Director) and Diane Kennedy

Wednesday 16th November

9.30	Pick-up from hotel to go to test facility
	with Diane Kennedy and Jasmine Goodman
10.00–3.00	Test facility tour
	with Jim Gibson (Test Manager)
4.00	Pick-up from office to airport
7.00	Flight departs to Australia

Minutes of the meeting

Date: June 27, 2011.
Time: 3.30-5.30
Place: Boardroom 3
Meeting objective: Diane Kennedy's visit to APU August 7-11
Present: Lowis Engineering: Dianne Kennedy (DK), Jasmine Goodman (JG),
Australian Power Utilities: John Carter (JC), Paul Rogers (PR)
Apologies: Lowis Engineering: Jennifer Williams (JW)

Points discussed

1. Trip schedule
DK to meet the APU Managing Director in Perth.
PR to confirm the trip to the APU Head Office in Sydney.
PR to send a schedule for the trip by August 1.

2. Travel arrangements
PR to arrange accommodation for DK.
JG to be responsible for travel arrangements.

3. AOB
JC to send the marketing plan by July 10.
DK to send feedback on the marketing plan by July 30.

Did you know?

在會議記錄裏，我們通常用 ...to do something 的結構。

Key words

Companies	
	Your translation
boss	
branch	
colleague	
department	
division	
employee	
employer	
headquarters	
job	
to manage	

Computers	
	Your translation
bug	
computer	
crash	
document	
drop-down menu	
error	
file	
keyboard	
LAN	
laptop	
monitor	
mouse	
patch	
password	
printer	
printer cartridge	
program	
pop-up	
software	
tablet	
virus	
Wi-Fi	
to delete	
to log off	
to log on	
to save	

Deliveries

	Your translation
address	
lorry (UK) / truck (US)	
package	
parcel	
registered post	
special delivery	
tracking number	
to delay	
to deliver	
to order	
to post	
to send	

Departments

	Your translation
Accounting	
Customer Services	
Distribution	
Human Resources	
Information Technology (IT)	
Logistics	
Marketing	
Payroll	
Production	
Research and Development	
Sales	
Security	
Transport	
Warehousing	

Key words

Events and meetings	
	Your translation
catering	
change	
conference room	
equipment	
event	
facilities	
flipchart	
invitation	
meeting room	
participant	
presentation	
projector	
to arrange	
to attend	
to book	
to bring forward	
to cancel	
to invite	
to organize	
to put / move back	
to reserve	

Industry	Your translation
advertising	
automotive / car	
aviation	
banking	
catering	
construction	
consumer electronics	
energy	
fashion	
food and drink	
healthcare	
insurance	
logistics	
telecommunications	
tourism	
pharmaceuticals	
public relations	
publishing	
retail	
waste disposal / management	
water	

Key words

In the office	Your translation
chair	
computer	
cubicle / work station	
desk	
fax machine	
hole punch (UK) / hole puncher (US)	
paper	
paper clip	
pen	
pencil	
photocopy (UK) / Xerox (US)	
print out	
stapler	
stationery	
telephone	
Xerox (US) / photocopy (UK)	
to fax	
to photocopy (UK) / to Xerox (US)	
to print something out	
to staple	
to Xerox (US) / to photocopy (UK)	

Office job titles

	Your translation
chairman / chairwoman	
chief executive officer	
chief financial officer	
clerk	
consultant	
engineer	
lawyer	
manager	
managing director	
personal assistant	
receptionist	
salesman / saleswoman / salesperson	
secretary	

Projects

	Your translation
budget	
client	
cost	
deadline	
delivery	
goal	
plan	
phase	
project	
project manager / member / team	
quality	
resources	
schedule	
status	
time	

Key words

Reception

	Your translation
appointment	
badge	
desk	
elevator (US) / lift (UK)	
entrance	
foyer	
guest	
seat	
security	
visitor	

Refreshments

	Your translation
biscuit (UK) / cookie (US)	
coffee	
cup	
glass	
juice	
milk	
mineral water	
sandwich	
sugar	
tea	

Telephone	
	Your translation
busy (line)	
cell (US) / mobile (UK) phone	
engaged (line) (UK)	
extension	
line	
to call	
to call back	
to connect *someone to someone*	
to hold (*the line*)	
to put *someone* through *to someone*	
to ring	

Travel	
	Your translation
flight	
hire car / car rental	
journey	
plane	
subway (US) / underground (UK)	
taxi	
tour	
traffic	
train	
trip	

Present simple 一般現在式

肯定形式：   I **work** on the reception desk.
            She **enjoys** her job very much.
            Our employees **love** helping visitors.

否定形式：   I **don't [do not] work** for Lowis Engineering.
            This visitor **doesn't [does not] have** a security card.
            We **don't allow** pets in the company.

提問：   **Does** she **work** for Lowis Engineering?
            Where **do** you **come** from?

長答案：   Yes, she **does work** for Lowis Engineering.
            No, she **doesn't work** for Lowis Engineering.

短答案：   Yes, I **do**.
            No, I **don't**.
            Yes, she **does**.
            No, she **doesn't**.

這種時態用於表達事實：

- Jasmine **works** at Lowis Engineering in London but she **lives** in Wimbledon.
- The office **is** on the corner of Wardour Street and Oxford Street.
- Diane **works** in London but she **comes** from Ireland.

和定期或例行活動：

- I **check** my emails every day.
- The postman **brings** the post before lunch.

它也在時間表或日程表內使用：

- The canteen **opens** at 12 o'clock.
- The company **closes** at midnight.

它也在 *if, when, until, as soon as* 和 *after* 的從句內使用：

- She'll give you her address *when* she **telephones**.
- I'll help you *after* I **finish** this report.
- We'll start the meeting *as soon as* the boss **arrives**.
- Let's wait *until* Paul **gets here**.

常用於一般現在式的詞語有：*often, seldom, usually, never, always, normally, rarely*：

- It **often** rains a lot in April.
- We **never** close.

Present continuous 現在進行式

肯定形式：	I'm [I am] **waiting** for my taxi. We're [We are] **staying** in the Anchor Hotel. They're [They are] **having** a meeting.
否定形式：	No, I'm not staying in the country. She isn't [She is not] **waiting** for Diane.
提問：	**Are** you **staying** at the Anchor Hotel? **Is** Mr Jones **waiting** to see me? When **are** they **leaving**?
長答案：	Yes. I'm staying at the Anchor. No, I'm not staying in London.
短答案：	Yes, I am. Yes, she is. Yes, they are. No, I'm not. No, she isn't. No, they aren't.

這種時態用於表達現在正在發生的動作：

- Would you like an umbrella because it's **raining** (now)?

或開始了但還未結束的動作：

- I'm **waiting** to see him.

也會用於短暫的行動或情況：

- She's **staying** at the Anchor Hotel in London for three nights.

它也可以有未來的含義，也可談及已經安排或計劃好的未來活動：

- I'm **staying** in the hotel next week too.

常用於現在進行式的詞語有：*now, at the moment, presently*

小心！這些動詞不常用於進行式：

> remember, understand, want, like, belong, suppose, need, seem, prefer,
> believe, know, think (= believe), hear, smell, have (= possess)

Grammar reference

Past simple 一般過去式

肯定形式：	He **arrived** yesterday. I **confirmed** my meeting last week. We **visited** the company last month. She **knew** there was a delay. We **ate** in the restaurant last night.
否定形式：	He **didn't [did not] telephone** yesterday. You **didn't tell** me that I would have to pay. They **didn't enjoy** their visit. I **didn't expect** to have to wait so long at reception.
提問：	**Did** Mr Lawson **arrive** yesterday? **Did** you **enjoy** your visit? **Did** the suppliers **receive** their money? What **did** you **buy** in London?
長答案：	Yes, he **arrived** yesterday. No, he **didn't arrive** yesterday. Yes, we **spoke** to the manager about your problem. No, we **didn't speak** to the manager about your problem.
短答案：	Yes, we **did**. No, we **didn't**. Yes, I **did**. No, I **didn't**.

這個時態用於過去已完成的動作：

- I **visited** your company last week.

或以往較長的情況：

- I **worked** at Siemens for 20 years.

常用於一般過去式的詞語有： *yesterday*、*an hour ago*、*last year*、*in 2009*、*last week*、*a year ago*。

Going to future　用 **going to** 表示未來

肯定形式：
I'm [I am] **going to send** an email tomorrow.
They're [They are] **going to complain** about the meeting.
He's [He is] **going to book** three conference rooms.
We're **going to write** to the manager.

否定形式：
I'm not [I am not] **going to telephone** tomorrow.
We aren't [We are not] **going to eat** in the restaurant tonight.
She **isn't going to go** to Australia.

提問：
Are you **going to telephone** tomorrow?
Is he **going to tell** the boss?
Who's **going to tell** the boss?

長答案：
Yes, I'm **going to telephone** tomorrow.
No, I'm **not going to telephone** tomorrow.
Yes, they're **going to email** the manager.
No, they **aren't going to email** the manager.

短答案：
Yes, I **am**.
No, I'm **not**.
Yes, he **is**.
No, he **isn't**.
Yes, they **are**.
No, they **aren't**.

這個時態用於表示已計劃或決定，並且肯定會發生的事：

- We're **going to move** offices next year.
- When **are** you **going to get** a company car?
- When I get home, I'm **going to write** a report about the conference.

Simple future – will 一般將來式 — will

肯定形式：	I**'ll** [I **will**] **post** it tomorrow.
	We**'ll arrange** a meeting.
	Sally**'ll call** me as soon as your taxi is here.
否定形式：	I **won't** [**will not**] **do** it tomorrow.
	Jasmine **won't forget** to do it, Paul.
	They **won't come** back.
提問：	**Will** you **do** it tomorrow?
	Will she **order** me a taxi?
	When **will** my taxi **come**?
長答案：	Yes, I**'ll do** it in a minute.
	No, I **won't do** it today.
短答案：	Yes, I will.
	No, I won't.

這個時態用於對將來的預測：

- In the year 2020 we**'ll** all **work** until we are 75.
- You**'ll** never **finish** that report before 1.00.

它也可用於提供關於未來的資訊 (但不包括意向或安排)：

- In ten minutes we**'ll test** the fire alarm.

它也可以在條件句內使用，例如 *if-* 句式：

- If you do not cancel in time, you**'ll have to** pay a fee.

它也可以用於回應提議的決定、承諾、威脅、請求、說明及建議：

- That sounds good. I**'ll have** the steak too.
- I**'ll tell** you as soon as the report is ready.
- I promise I**'ll** inform my boss immediately.
- Do that again and I**'ll complain** your boss.
- **Will** you **fill** in this form, please?

Present perfect simple 一般現在完成式

肯定形式：	I**'ve** [I **have**] **worked here** for ten years.
	She**'s** [She **has**] **done** secretarial work for ten years.
	The manager **has read** your letter.
否定形式：	I **haven't** [**have not**] **worked** in an office before.
	She **hasn't** [**has not**] **ordered** a taxi.
提問：	**Have** you **worked** in London before?
	Has my taxi **been** ordered?
	Where **have** you **put** the brochures?
長答案：	Yes, I**'ve worked** in London for five years.
	No, I **haven't** [**have not**] **ordered** a taxi.
短答案：	Yes, I **have**.
	No, I **haven't**.
	Yes, it **has**.
	No, it **hasn't**.

這個時態用於描述過去已完成，但和現在有關的動作：

- Can you help me? I**'ve lost** the key to my office. (= I don't have it.)
- We have to cancel our visit because she's **broken** her leg. (= Her leg is broken.)
- I**'ve read** some information about your company. (= I know about the company.)
- We**'ve moved** offices since your last visit. (= The offices are different.)

> 記住談及某事發生時，若含標示完成時間的詞語或詞組，如：yesterday、last week、at 10 o'clock this morning、in 2010 及 last October 等，就不會用現在完成式。

- I'm sure we**'ve met** before!
- **Have** you ever **stayed** in the Anchor Hotel before?
- My boss **has been** to a conference here.
- The hotel **has been** in the Anchor Group for over 25 years.

它也用於描述某些事情"時間流逝至現在"。提示詞語有：*just*、*yet*、*already*。

- **Have you sent** the report **yet**?
- She**'s just finished** the email.
- We**'ve just received** a phone call from Paul Rogers.
- I**'ve already ordered** Mrs Wilson's coffee.

Infinitive	Past simple	Past participle	Infinitive	Past simple	Past participle
be	was	been	meet	met	met
become	became	become	pay	paid	paid
blow	blew	blown	put	put	put
break	broke	broken	read	read	read
bring	brought	brought	ring	rang	rung
build	built	built	rise	rose	risen
buy	bought	bought	run	ran	run
choose	chose	chosen	say	said	said
come	came	come	see	saw	seen
cost	cost	cost	sell	sold	sold
cut	cut	cut	send	sent	sent
do	did	done	show	showed	shown
drink	drank	drunk	shut	shut	shut
drive	drove	driven	sit	sat	sat
eat	ate	eaten	speak	spoke	spoken
fall	fell	fallen	spend	spent	spent
find	found	found	stand	stood	stood
fly	flew	flown	steal	stole	stolen
get	got	got / gotten (US)	stick	stuck	stuck
give	gave	given	swim	swam	swum
have	had	had	take	took	taken
hear	heard	heard	teach	taught	taught
hide	hid	hidden	tell	told	told
hold	held	held	think	thought	thought
keep	kept	kept	understand	understood	understood
know	knew	known	wear	wore	worn
lead	led	led	win	won	won
learn	learned	learned	write	wrote	written
leave	left	left			
lend	lent	lent			
let	let	let			
make	made	made			
mean	meant	meant			

a/c	account
am	to show the time is between midnight and noon
AGM	annual general meeting
AOB	any other business
approx	approximately
asap	as soon as possible
bcc	blind copied to
cc	copied to
CEO	chief executive officer
FAO	for the attention of
FAQ	frequently asked question
Inc	incorporated
Ltd	limited
N/A	not applicable
NB	pay particular attention to this
PA	personal assistant
p.a.	per annum (per year)
pm	to show the time is between noon and midnight
PR	public relations
PTO	please turn over
p.w.	per week
qty	quantity
R&D	research and development
re	with reference to
RSVP	please reply (French: répondez s'il vous plaît)
VAT	value added tax
WWW	world wide web

How do I say ... ?

Dates	
You write	**You say**
Monday 18 August (especially UK)	Monday, the eighteenth of August
Monday, August 18 (US)	Monday, August (the) eighteenth
2011	two thousand and eleven *OR* twenty eleven
2/11/2011 (UK)	the second of November, two thousand and eleven *OR* twenty eleven
11/2/2011 (US)	November the second, two thousand and eleven *OR* twenty eleven
October 3rd (US)	October (the) third
3rd October (UK)	the third of October

- 在英式英語裏，通常時間的讀寫方法是：日 / 月 / 年。
- 在美式英語裏，通常時間的讀寫方法是：月 / 日 / 年。

Times	
The time is....	**You say**
09.15	nine fifteen *OR* quarter past nine *OR* quarter after nine (US)
10.00	ten o'clock (in the morning) *OR* ten am
22.00 (UK)	ten o'clock (in the evening) *OR* ten pm
11.30	eleven thirty *OR* half past eleven
14.40	fourteen forty (UK) *OR* two forty in the afternoon *OR* twenty to three
16.20	sixteen twenty *OR* twenty past four (in the afternoon) *OR* twenty after four (US)
16.21	sixteen twenty one *OR* twenty one minutes past four
15.00	fifteen hundred (hours) *OR* three o'clock (in the afternoon)
17.45	seventeen forty-five *OR* quarter to six

- 在美式英語裏，不會用二十四小時時制。例如：22:00 是 10 pm，而10:00 是 10 am。

Time	
1.5 hours	ninety minutes *OR* one and a half hours *OR* an hour and a half
15 minutes	fifteen minutes *OR* quarter of an hour
30 minutes	thirty minutes *OR* half an hour
45 minutes	forty five minutes *OR* three quarters of an hour

- 在英式英語裏，二十四小時時制　(16:45 = sixteen forty five) 主要用來説鐵路和航班時間。而在美式英語裏，二十四小時時制的用法很罕見。
- 我們通常不會在日常對話裏用二十四小時時制　(16:45 = sixteen forty five)。例如，我們不會説：*The meeting will start at fifteen hundred hours*，而是説 *The meeting will start at three pm / at three o'clock*。

Prices	
You write	**You say**
£10.99	ten pounds ninety-nine (pence)
€140.00	one hundred (and) forty euros
$22.90	twenty-two (dollars) (and) ninety (cents)
£87.00	eighty-seven pounds

Telephone numbers	
The telephone number is:	**You say:**
0044 171 200 3612	double oh, double four, one seven one, two double oh, three six one two (UK)
0044 171 200 3612	zero zero four four, one seven one, two zero zero, three six one two (US)
020 677 3219	oh two oh six double seven, three two one nine
ex: 5640	extension five six four oh (UK)
ex: 5640	extension five six four zero / oh (US)

- 在美式英語裏，通常不會説 double four 或 treble four，而是説 four、four 或 four、four、four。
- 你可以用 oh 或 zero 表示 "零"。在美式英語裏，較常使用 zero。

Email addresses and websites	
The email address is:	**You say:**
jasmine.goodman@lowis.com	jasmine dot goodman at Lowis dot com
The website address is:	**You say:**
www.lowisengineering.com/aboutus	www dot lowis engineering dot com forward slash about us

用英語講電話時，可以使用以下短語句子。何不將這兩頁影印下來，然後放在電話附近方便查閱？

52
CD

Asking to speak to someone on the phone 請求和某人通話

- Could I speak to _____, please?
- Can I speak to _____, please?
- Could you put me through to _____, please?
- I'm trying to contact _____.
- I'm trying to get in touch with _____.
- I'm trying to get hold of _____.

Asking for identification on the phone 詢問對方的身份

- Who's calling, please?
- Who's speaking?
- Who shall I say is calling?
- Could I have your name (again), please?
- Could you give me your name, please?
- I'm sorry I didn't quite catch / get your name.
- Would you mind spelling that (your name / first name / surname) for me?
- Could you spell that for me?

Asking for repetition / clarification on the phone 請對方在電話中重複或解釋

- I'm sorry, I didn't quite catch / get that. Could you repeat it?
- I'm afraid that was a little (bit) too fast. Would you mind repeating it more slowly for me?
- I didn't understand the last word of the address. Could you give it to me again?
- Is that Mr Smith or Mrs?
- I'm sorry, did you say Oxford Road or Oxford Parade?
- I beg your pardon? / Pardon?
- Sorry?
- I'm (very) sorry. I'm not familiar with English / French / Japanese surnames. Could you spell that for me?
- Could you repeat that a little more slowly, please?

 You may photocopy these pages.

Asking the caller to wait 請來電者稍等

- Hold the line, please.
- Please hold the line.
- Would you (just) hold the line a moment, please?
- (Just) One moment, please. I'm just putting you through to that room / department.
- Could you hold on a moment, please?
- Could you wait a moment, please?
- One moment, please. I'll be with you in a second.

Answering the phone 接聽電話

- Good morning, Lowis Engineering. Simon speaking. How can I help you?
- Good morning, Lowis Engineering. Simon speaking. How may I direct your call?

Offering to help 提供協助

- I'm sorry, the line's busy. Can I help?
- I'm sorry, there's no one answering. Can I take a message?
- Would you like to leave a message?

The aviation alphabet 核對拼寫的字母表

請用以下的詞語去核對拼寫。

My name's Mr Whyte – that's W for Whisky, H for Hotel, Y for Yankee, T for Tango and E for Echo.

A for Alpha	G for Golf	M for Mike	S for Sierra	Y for Yankee
B for Bravo	H for Hotel	N for November	T for Tango	Z for Zulu
C for Charlie	I for India	O for Oscar	U for Uniform	
D for Delta	J for Juliet	P for Papa	V for Victor	
E for Echo	K for Kilo	Q for Quebec	W for Whisky	
F for Foxtrot	L for Lima	R for Romeo	X for X-Ray	

記住在美式英語裏，Z 讀作 zee；而在英式英語裏則讀作 zed。

You may photocopy these pages.

Notes